One Small Lost Sheep

Farrar Straus Giroux

New York

One Small Lost Sheep

CLAUDIA MILLS Pictures by WALTER LYON KRUDOP

Text copyright © 1997 by Claudia Mills
Illustrations copyright © 1997 by Walter Lyon Krudop
All rights reserved
Published simultaneously in Canada by HarperCollinsCanadaLtd
Color separations by Hong Kong Scanner Arts
Printed in the United States of America by Berryville Graphics
Designed by Lilian Rosenstreich
First edition, 1997

Library of Congress Cataloging-in-Publication Data
Mills, Claudia.
  One small lost sheep / Claudia Mills ; pictures by Walter
Lyon Krudop.—1st ed.
    p. cm.
    Summary: While looking for Kivsa, his lame sheep,
Benjamin misses the wondrous announcement that the angels
make to the other shepherds near Bethlehem, but it is Kivsa
who leads him to the newborn king.
    ISBN 0-374-35649-1
    [1. Shepherds—Fiction. 2. Jesus Christ—Nativity—Fiction.]
I. Krudop, Walter, ill. II. Title.
PZ7.M639630p   1997
[E]—dc20   96-18609

To Gregory and Christopher —C. M.

To T. B. —W. L. K.

A long time ago, on a starlit night, a little shepherd boy named Benjamin was out in the windy hills above Bethlehem searching for one small lost sheep.

The rest of his father's sheep huddled safely together, near the other sheep watched over by the other shepherds. But Benjamin's own, best-loved lamb, lame from birth, had strayed from the flock.

Benjamin scrambled over the rocky hillside, calling her name. "Kivsa! Kivsa!"

Brambles tore at Benjamin's bare knees, but he kept on climbing. "Kivsa!"

He thought he saw some white wool up ahead and hurried toward it. But it was only a piece of rough-woven cloth, dropped by some passing shepherd.

Where could Kivsa be? So many dangers could befall a
small sheep all alone in the night. The rocks were slippery
and jagged; even a sheep who wasn't lame might stumble.
Hungry wolves lay in wait. A large hawk might attack a
lone sheep, helpless and unprotected.

Benjamin struggled not to cry. He had taken care of Kivsa since her birth. As a sickly newborn, she had sucked on his fingers, dipped in milk. From then on, she had followed him everywhere, limping behind him almost as quickly as if her crooked hind leg had been strong and straight. At night she'd slept curled next to him, so that he felt her warmth through his tunic.

Benjamin pressed on, hardly knowing where to look. His legs were scratched and bleeding from thorns and thistles. In the sky above, one star shone brighter than the rest. But its light didn't lead him to Kivsa.

"Kiv!" Benjamin called once more.

Then he dropped down onto the nearest rock and wrapped his arms around his knees. He cried until he fell asleep.

When Benjamin awoke, the night seemed different
somehow. The sky was oddly light, yet Benjamin
sensed that dawn was still far away.

He rose and began to trudge back to his family.

Maybe Kivsa had found her own way there by now.

When he finally reached the shepherds, one glance told him: No, Kivsa had not returned.

"Benjamin!" His oldest brother, David, came running to meet him.
"Did you see it?"

"Kivsa? I couldn't find her."

"No, the stars! And the sky—it opened up! And there were angels!
Singing the most beautiful song."

Benjamin stared at his brother. He had never seen David so excited.

Bewildered, he shook his head. "I fell asleep. I didn't see anything. I didn't hear anything."

"A whole chorus of angels, singing just to us! I can't believe you missed it," David said.

"Well, I did," Benjamin said crossly. It seemed so unfair—to have lost Kivsa, and then to have slept through such wonderment.

The others crowded around Benjamin, telling the same astonishing story that David had told.

Benjamin interrupted them. "You haven't seen Kivsa, have you?"

No one listened. No one but Benjamin seemed to care about one small lost sheep.

"The angels brought news that a king was born," Benjamin's father told him. "Just now! In Bethlehem! A king in our own village!"

"We must go to see him at once!" a man called out.

More voices took up the cry. "We must go to see the new king!"

The shepherds began heading down the hillside, rousing their sleeping sheep to follow. Benjamin let the crowd carry him along, but as he went, he strained his eyes for a glimpse of Kivsa.

When they reached Bethlehem, the shepherds stopped, as if uncertain where to go.

"The angels said we would find the king in a stable," Benjamin's father said. "But which one? There are so many stables in Bethlehem." He sounded almost angry.

Suddenly Benjamin's heart clenched like a fist. From the distance, he'd heard the bleat of a young sheep. Could it be Kivsa?

Benjamin pushed past
the others and ran on
ahead, down the dark
street lit by the strangely
bright star. He heard a
second soft baa, turned
the corner, and then saw
her, not ten feet away, in
a broken-down stable.

Kivsa stood next to a wooden manger that seemed to glow, as if all the stars in the heavens had given it their light. Beside her stood other animals Benjamin recognized from the village. Isaiah's blind ox, his massive, sightless head bent low. A half-starved donkey, beaten and neglected by his master. An old goat, stooped with age, missing one ear.

Benjamin drew close to Kivsa, his throat thick with tears of joy.

Then he saw the newborn baby lying in the
manger, warmed by the breath of the animals
gathered there. Behind the manger, he saw a
man and a woman, too. They smiled at Benjamin,
a gentle, welcoming smile.

Wordlessly, Benjamin dropped to his knees. He knew, without any angels to tell him, that this was the newborn king.

Then the other shepherds were behind him, kneeling, too.

Kivsa crept beneath the folds of Benjamin's cloak. She lay quiet, her breath soft and warm against his chest. Benjamin heard the angels now, but this time they were singing inside his heart.

getting ready

general information
beaded crochet

The basic idea of beaded crochet is to create a fiber tube of crochet in which the beads land on the outside of the tube. Through a series of specific steps, the fiber is crocheted with the beads in certain positions in the process. Seed beads are the most popular type used; but many other kinds of beads can be used, especially in combination with seed beads. Crystals, pearls, semiprecious beads, all are wonderful additions to the basic rope, either within the rope itself or as embellishments. Natural fibers such as cotton and silk are appropriate in certain weights, but polyesters, nylons, rayons, and metallics work wonderfully. Ropes can be combined, joined, braided, and stiffened with wire. Let your imagination run wild!

beads

Theoretically, all the different sizes of seed beads can be used in beaded crochet. The key to succeeding in working with any size of seed bead is to match the size of the crochet hook and the weight of the fiber so the design will work. Another factor that may affect the outcome of your pattern is the number of beads in the basic round; a tube crocheted of six around will work with just about any size bead, but a tube of twelve around would be cumbersome in the largest and smallest sizes of beads. In practice, the most commonly used sizes of seed beads are 15o, delica beads and Treasures, 11o, 8o, and 6o.

15o seed beads

12o three-cut seed beads

Delica/Treasure beads

11o seed beads

8o seed beads

6o seed beads

15o Seed Beads

Japanese 15o seed beads work up wonderfully in tube crochet. You must use a fine fiber such as topstitching thread or beading nylon. The #15, #14 and #13 hooks work well for this size bead. You can try using a #12 hook as well.

12o Three-cut Beads

These delightful little "faceted" seed beads add wonderful sparkle to any pattern. Use topstitching thread or beading nylon, and a #12 or #13 crochet hook.

Delica Beads & Treasures

These little cylinders come in an astonishing range of colors and finishes. However, when creating a tube, their precisely cylindrical shape can be more of a problem than an asset. The squared-off shape limits the ability of the tube to bend. They are very useful in patterns where graduated sizes are needed, to bridge the gap between an 11o seed bead and smaller beads as is done in the Black Beauty Set on pages 66–68. Use topstitching thread or beading nylon and a #11 or #12 hook.

11o Seed Beads

These are the standard. There are many different manufacturers of seed beads in this size from all parts of the world. Japanese seed beads tend to be very regular and consistent in their size. They are often slightly larger than Czech 11o seed beads, which are a bit more irregular in shape. Some beaders prefer not to mix the two, but in this book they are often used together. In patterns where graduated sizes are required, you can actually use some Czech 11o beads as a smaller size than Japanese 11o beads.

There are literally thousands of colors and finishes available from the different manufacturers. Use #12 perle cotton, topstitching thread, or beading nylon and a #10, #11 or #12 hook. The 11o beads are also available in hex and cut styles as well; they can be mixed successfully with the regular 11o beads. Cut beads often have flat tops like delicas and bugle beads, so bendability may be an issue if you work an entire pattern using them; their best use is in mixing with other beads as accents.

8o Seed Beads

These beads are the same as 11o beads, but slightly larger. The 8o beads are available in different shapes such as hex and triangles as well. The range of colors is similar to that of 11o beads, but availability is more of an issue. Use topstitching thread, #8 or #10 perle cotton, silks, rayons, and metallics with these beads. A #10 or #11 hook will work well.

6o Seed Beads

Big and beautiful! These are wonderful for use in ropes that are more substantial. They make wonderful roll-on bangles and can be successfully mixed with other sizes of beads, especially seed pearls and 3mm–4mm faceted fire-polish beads.

Special Beads for Crochet

Faceted fire-polish beads are great for tube crochet, especially in the smaller sizes (3mm and 4mm). Clear faceted beads can be combined with bright colors of nylon or silk to create truly luminous pieces such as the Pretty in Pink Set on pages 69–71. When combined with seed beads such as in the Stardust Bracelet on pages 63–65, they add glamour to a pattern. Follow the same rules for fibers, needles, and hooks as for size 8o seed beads.

Seed pearls, small round genuine fresh-water pearls in sizes 2.5mm–4mm, work up very nicely. They were used frequently in the Victorian era to create pearl ropes; many wonderful examples survive, but some have perished due to fiber rot since the synthetic fibers that last forever were not available during Victoria's heyday. The critical issue with pearls is the size of the hole, which is often very small, requiring a size 12 threading needle and beading nylon. You will find that a few pearls on a strand simply are not usable for that reason. Make certain to purchase more than you think you will need to complete the pattern.

Cut crystal can also be used, but beware—the edges of cut crystal are sharp and may cut the thread. Because crochet puts a good amount of stress on the thread, it will be more prone to cutting than in normal beading use. Use cut crystals carefully.

Throughout this book, other shapes and sizes of beads are used in tubular crochet such as in the Island Princess Bracelet on pages 72–73. With so many options, there is plenty of room for experimentation. Do not hesitate to substitute your own bead choices for those that are called for in the instructions.

fibers & things

There are several fibers available that are suitable for beaded crochet. Fiber selection is largely determined by weight and color and depends on the type and size of beads you will be using in the pattern.

Perle Cotton

Perle Cotton

Perle cotton is made by several different manufacturers. Each produces a tremendous range of available colors. There are four weights frequently used in tubular crochet. The #5 is used mainly with larger beads such as 6o seed beads and pony beads. It is also used in designs where unbeaded crochet stitches are visible. Use a #9 or larger crochet hook with #5 perle cotton. The #8 perle cotton is often used in the same manner as its slightly larger counterpart, but #8 can be used with smaller beads such as 8o seed beads, as well.

Perhaps the most useful size is #10 perle cotton, especially if you will be using 8o seed beads and 11o seed beads to complete the bulk of the project. The #10 perle cotton can be threaded with a #10 beading needle. It is easier to see than topstitching thread and can be easily substituted in most projects (except those that call for 15o beads and pearls) if the stitcher has vision impairments. The #12 perle cotton, the finest size that can reasonably be used for crochet, may be used with 11o seed beads and, in some cases, 15o seed beads.

Perle Cotton Comparisons

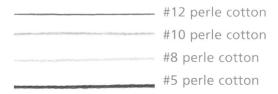

——————————————— #12 perle cotton
——————————————— #10 perle cotton
——————————————— #8 perle cotton
——————————————— #5 perle cotton

Take care to avoid splitting the thread when crocheting with perle cotton. If the project will be exposed to moisture or excessive wear, it may be better to use polyester topstitching thread or beading nylon as the base fiber.

Variegated colors, both monotone and multicolored, are widely available in perle cotton. Try combining a base color of perle cotton with matte transparent beads to yield interesting results. For example, in the Blue Jeans Set on pages 34–36, the color of the perle cotton is actually deep navy, and the bead is light blue. However, when combined they produce a wonderful denim look that neither the bead or the fiber has on its own.

Nylon Beading Threads

The heavier weights of nylon beading thread are excellent for use in tubular crochet. Sizes F and G are good choices for use with beads that have very small holes, such as pearls and semiprecious stones. They resist wear, especially if the fiber is waxed prior to use. They are unaffected by moisture and cosmetics, and are so thin that they are virtually invisible in the finished tube. Like topstitching thread, beading nylon is a good choice where beads of different sizes and shapes are combined in one project.

The range of colors in beading nylon is more limited than in other types of fibers, but the basics—black, white, ivory, gold, and gray—can be found without too much difficulty.

Just about any threading needle can be used with nylon. However, these threads are more prone to splitting than other types of thread, so be mindful of that as you crochet.

Rayon & Silk Threads

What beautiful fibers! The natural sheen of rayon and silk threads can be incorporated into crochet designs in so many ways. The luminescence shows through transparent beads, producing an almost "neon" effect such as you will find in the Pretty in Pink Set. If you use transparent beads with a colored lining, some of the fiber will show through, such as in the Tiger Lily Necklace on pages 46–48 and the Snow Queen Necklace on pages 42–43.

Rayon Threads

Rayon and silk can bc difficult to handle; thread management is something of an issue in projects using either of these fibers. When threading beads onto these fibers, take care to let the beads fall naturally on the thread if possible; if you push them too firmly against the thread, you may damage it. It is quite likely that you will have to trim off the first several inches of thread at the needle end before you begin crocheting.

Silk Threads

Topstitching Threads

Rayon and silk have a tendency to unwind spontaneously from a spool or cone, so take a moment to transfer the thread to a winding card before you begin threading the beads. Overestimate the amount you will need; because of the slippery nature of the fiber, pulling in a new thread can be tricky.

Splitting can also be a problem with rayon and silk. Use the largest size crochet hook that will produce the desired result. The smaller the hook end, the more likely it is that you will push the hook right through the fiber itself. If a section of your fiber becomes frayed, you may have to cut out a section and pull in a new thread, so try to avoid ripping out.

Topstitching Threads

These are good all-around threads for use in tubular crochet because it has some substance and strength. A 100% polyester thread is recommended because it is impervious to damage from water or cosmetics, and because it resists fraying and splitting. This weight of thread can be used with very small beads such as 15o seed beads, but will take the weight of 6o seed beads and larger round beads without breaking.

There is a wonderful range of colors available. Keep an assortment of neutrals including gray, gold, white, black, and ivory—you can do almost any project with that selection.

Select a needle for threading with topstitching thread according to the size of the bead. As always, use the largest needle that your beads will accommodate. Topstitching thread will easily fit through the eye of a #12 beading needle.

Metallic Fibers

Metallic braids are wonderful for chain-stitch patterns such as the Sparkly Bracelet on pages 122–123 and the Confetti Necklace on pages 124–125. They have a natural tendency to "kink" that can be incorporated into the design with great results. The kink will be minimized if the beads are too heavy; but if you use relatively small or lightweight beads, the kink will be maintained.

Transparent crystal beads are excellent for use with metallic fibers because the shine of the fiber will show through, such as in the Tea Party Necklace on pages 105–107. Variegated colors are especially beautiful when used with transparent crystal beads.

Use the smallest-eyed needle possible for threading beads onto metallic fibers. Use a #28 or #26 tapestry needle to accommodate the thickness of the braid. Take care to avoid splitting the thread with the hook while crocheting—a common hazard when working with braids. Also, take care to avoid letting the thread become worn or frayed.

Metallic fibers

Note: For tubular crochet, make certain to use medium-weight metallic braids—blending filaments and fine unbraided metallic fibers may be combined with other, stronger fiber, but are too lightweight to stand the strain of tubular crochet on their own.

Wires

You can crochet with the lighter gauges of wire—28-gauge and 34-gauge—in much the same manner as thread. If you keep in mind a few guidelines, your experience with wire can be very pleasant.

Crocheting a tube with wire produces an almost identical result as with thread; but surprisingly, the tube will be every bit as flexible as the thread tube, so it will not hold a specific shape as you might expect unless the wire is 22-gauge or heavier. A 34-gauge wire is wonderful when you are working with beads with very fine holes that have trouble accommodating the combination of needle and thread such as pearls, citrine, garnet, tourmaline, peridot, and other clear gemstone beads. Wire, on the other hand, easily slips through the holes.

Use good-quality wire when crocheting; burrs and kinks can be a nightmare. Colored wires often have a coating that makes the surface smoother. The quality of the wire is especially important if any of it will be left showing as part of the design.

The process of crocheting with wire puts a much greater strain on your hands than crocheting with thread. You may find that your hands will tire more quickly, so take a break every now and then to give your hands a rest.

When working with thread, it is quite easy to take the slack out of the stitch at nearly any point. With wire, the slack needs to be taken out of the loop on the hook before you pull the wire through to form a new loop. Once you have pulled up the new loop, it will be virtually impossible to change the loop that was originally on the hook.

Once you have threaded the beads onto the wire, roll it around something that is circular in shape, such as an empty roll from paper towels or toilet paper. Doing so will help prevent kinking of the wire. Although kinking will not ruin your design, it will make it more difficult to do the stitching because it will make it more difficult to slip the beads over the wire as you work.

If the wire breaks while you are working, you can add a new wire in the same manner as you would add a thread; pull a new loop through the existing loop and continue as if the wire had not broken. When you have progressed a few beads into the pattern, work the wire ends back into the crochet to hide them.

tools

There are just a few tools that are necessary for completing the designs in this book. You will need crochet hooks, pliers, threading needles, winding cards, wire cutters, and a pair of small sharp scissors.

Crochet Hooks

Having the right size crochet hook is essential to successfully working each design. Make certain to keep on hand a collection of steel crochet hooks sized #10–#14.

Crochet Hook Comparisons

#14 steel hook

#13 steel hook

#12 steel hook

#11 steel hook

#10 steel hook

Pliers

Round-nosed pliers are used mainly for bending wire and forming loops in head pins. Needle-nosed pliers are used for closing loops, flattening crimps, and attaching rings.

Threading Needles

You will begin each beaded crochet design by threading a fiber onto a beading needle and using it to put all the beads for the pattern on the fiber. You should have an assortment of beading needles, including tapestry needles in #24, #26, and #28, a #9 embroidery needle, and short beading needles in #10 and #12.

Threading Needle Comparisons

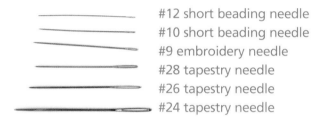

#12 short beading needle

#10 short beading needle

#9 embroidery needle

#28 tapestry needle

#26 tapestry needle

#24 tapestry needle

Winding Cards

Winding cards can be made in any size from lightweight cardboard, using the design shown here. The two holes will hold your hook with the loop still in place.

Winding Card

Wire Cutters

Wire cutters are used for trimming head pins, eye pins, and beading wire. These can be found at hardware stores.

threading beads

First on, last off—that's the way it works. The first bead you put on the thread will be the last one crocheted. Threading on a simple pattern is easy, often mindless, but the complex patterns can be a challenge.

It is useful, if you have room in your work area, to lay out small piles of beads in the same order as your threading pattern. Doing so will enable you to pick up one bead from each pile in order.

Counting from Patterns

If you are reading a pattern from a chart, make certain you understand the threading order before you begin. In *Beaded Crochet Designs*, we offer both pattern overview diagrams in stacked diagonal charts, and pattern detail diagrams, shown in rows of rounds.

Read a Pattern Overview Diagram beginning at the bottom row, and work from left to right, upward by rows, always reading each row from left to right.

Pattern Overview Diagram

Diagrams should be counted from left to right, starting at the bottom and working upward.

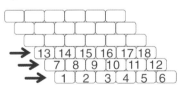

A Pattern Detail Diagram also should be read from left to right, but start at the top row and work downward through the rows. Each round is grouped separately, showing the number of beads in each round.

Pattern Detail Diagram

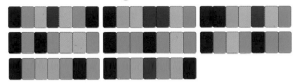

Diagrams should be counted from left to right, starting at the top row and working downward.

Marking Rounds & Checking Repeats

When threading on a complex pattern with multiple rounds per repeat, it is useful to mark the end of each round with a small square of lightweight paper. (Fig. 1) After threading on the first repeat, check it carefully for accuracy, then use it to compare each successive repeat to the original. If you find an error within the last few beads, simply remove the beads to the point of the error and redo the threading.

Fig. 1

Place a small paper marker between multiple rounds in a repeat.

If you find an error far back in the threading, place a thread marker in that spot, then slip-stitch without a bead at the error marker in the crocheting. (Fig. 2) Later, go back and add the required bead with a needle and thread so the pattern will be complete.

Fig. 2

tube crochet

Follow the step-by-step instructions in the order shown below to create a beaded crochet tube of six beads around. If you are crocheting a tube of more than six beads around, adjust these instructions accordingly.

1. Following the pattern detail diagram for the project, place a needle on the end of the thread and load all the beads onto the thread. (Fig. 1)

Hint: If you are using only one bead color, pour the beads into a container and scoop the needle through the beads. If you are loading in a specific pattern, arrange the beads in small adjacent piles in the correct order.

2. Make a slipknot on the hook. (Fig. 2)

3. Make six chain stitches, each with one bead. (Fig. 3)

4. Insert the hook into the first beaded chain, then slide the bead over to the far side of the hook. (Fig. 4 on page 19)

Note: This is an important step; in order for the entire process to be successful, all the beads must "land" on the outside of the tube.

5. Slide a bead down the thread so it sits directly on top of the bead you just moved to the far

(Fig. 4 on page 19)

Fig. 1

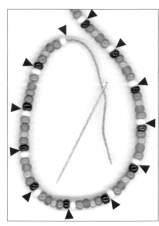

Above: Loaded beads rolled onto the spool. *Right:* Beads loaded in a specific repeat.

Fig. 2

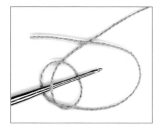
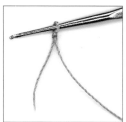

Position the hook in a loop of thread, then pull so the slipknot forms on the hook.

Fig. 3

Above: To chain with a bead, slide a bead down the thread until it hangs below the hook. *Above right:* Wrap the thread around the hook and pull it through the loop. *Right:* Six chained beads.

Fig. 4

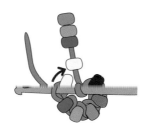

Fig. 5

If you have created a pattern of six beads in repeat as shown, the bead that you slide down the thread will be the same color as the bead you just moved to the far side of the tube. This will happen with each new "pair" of beads, the one you have crocheted, and the one you slide down the thread.

Fig. 6

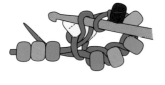

Fig. 7

Fig. 8

Note that the next beaded stitch into which you will insert the hook has a cream bead, which is the color of the next bead you will slide down the thread.

Fig. 9

The lower beads are positioned horizontally, while the beads of the new round are somewhat vertical.

side of the hook. The thread should come from the right of the bead you just moved to the far side of the hook. When the bead is properly positioned, wrap the thread over the hook. (Fig. 5)

6. You now have two loops on the hook and the thread is wrapped around the hook. Pull the thread through the first loop. You will have two loops on the hook when this step is complete. (Fig. 6)

7. Pull the first loop through the second loop. This completes the stitch. (Fig. 7)

8. Repeat Steps 4–7 until you have six completed stitches. This completes the first round of six. Flatten the work; from above, you should already see six "spokes" of thread. At the end of each spoke is one bead. (Fig. 8) Seen from the side, the beads will show the beginning stages of a spiral pattern even at this early stage. (Fig. 9) As the tube lengthens, the spiral pattern will become more visible, and the relative positioning of the beads (horizontal, vertical) will be more pronounced. (Fig. 10)

Fig. 10

Troubleshooting Tube Crochet Problems

You do not have six beads in the round you are working on:

After every few rounds, check the tube to be sure there are six beads around the spokes

when you flatten the top. Fig. 11
If you see less or more
than six, pull out the work
until there are six. You
have either missed one
stitch or placed more than
one bead into a stitch.
(Fig. 11)

A bead appears in the center of the tube:

If you look at the side Fig. 12
of the tube, one bead
seems to be receding. (Fig.
12) If you look at the top
of the tube, a bead is in
the center of the spokes.
This could mean that the

bead you moved to the far side of the hook has
slipped through as you pulled the thread
through the loops. It may also mean that the
wrapped thread did not come from the right of
the bead on the hook. If this happens, you can
either push the bead back out again, or pull out
stitches until the work looks correct again.

finishing

Making an Invisible Join

Note: In these diagrams, the blue beads indicate the last round crocheted, and the pale pink beads indicate the first round crocheted.

1. If you are working in a pattern, ascertain that
the beginning and end of the tube you wish to
join invisibly are "in pattern" with each other;
in other words, if you continued to crochet

using the beads of the first Fig. 1
round, the pattern would
be correct. (Fig. 1) When
you are satisfied that this is
the case, cut the end thread
(shown in red), leaving a
12" tail, and secure it by
running it through the last
loop on the hook. Place a
needle on the starting thread
tail and bury it within the
tube by running the needle
into and through the fibers of the tube.

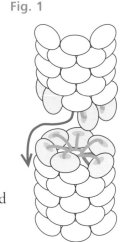

Note: Take care not to run the tail thread through the center holes of the beads, or the tube will be distorted.

Place the end thread tail on a needle. Align
the end and start of the tube.

2. Run the Fig. 2
needle through
the thread path
shown. (Fig. 2)
The dark blue
dots indicate
the thread that
holds each bead
in place on the
tube.

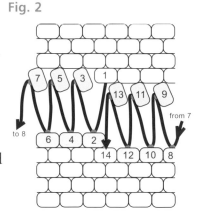

Note: The thread must follow this specific path for the joint to appear seamless.

3. As the work progresses, draw tube ends close
together and take out the slack in the thread.

The beads of the end round (blue) will shift into the horizontal position, and appear to be attached to the beads of the beginning round (light pink). (Fig. 3, Bead 3.) Continue around the tube until the two ends are firmly joined and in proper alignment.

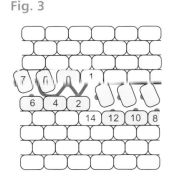

Fig. 3

4. Secure the excess thread within the weave, taking care to run the thread only through the fibers and not through the bead holes. When you are certain that the thread is secure, cut off the excess, taking care not to cut any of the threads that hold beads.

Finishing with Focal Bead

A bangle bracelet made with tubular crochet can be finished with a focal bead, either with or without bead caps. You also can use more than one bead, if desired. It is a good idea to keep the span of the focal beads less than one-fourth the size of the entire bracelet.

If you are using bead caps, you should draw in the beads at the finishing end of the tube—the beads at the start will already be somewhat drawn in. To do this, simply run a thread through the last round of beads and pull it so the beads draw inward. To flatten the end of the tube prior to finishing, simply make a slip stitch without a bead in all the beads of the last round. (Fig. 4) The beads will lie flat in the same manner as those of the previous rounds

(beads shown in green). Secure the ending thread within the fibers of the tube and trim the excess. If you are creating a piece without bead caps, this is an effective way to finish the end of the tube. Again, the beginning of the tube will look the same.

Fig. 4

Use a strong nylon beading thread to bridge the gap between the ends of the tube. A long rigid needle is helpful. Secure the nylon thread within the fibers of the tube on either end of the tube and bring the thread out from the center of the tube end. (Fig. 5)

Fig. 5

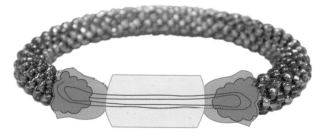

Add the caps and focal bead and run the nylon thread into the center of the other end of the tube. Pull gently but firmly until all the slack is taken out of the nylon. At this point, you should secure the nylon in position by running the needle back in the opposite direction. Repeat this running of thread from one end of the tube through the focal beads and into the other end of the tube several times until the focal bead and caps are secure and the tube ends are covered.

If you are not using caps, you will need to make one round of unbeaded slip stitches at the finishing end of the tube. This will "flatten" the beads in the last round so they look the same as the beads of the first round.

Repeat the same procedure used for caps and focal bead, but omit the caps.

Joining Two Tube Ends to Reduce to One

1. Complete the tube crochet to the desired length. Bind off the last stitch of the working end, then bury the thread tails from both ends in the fibers of the tube.

2. Position the two ends together so the last stitch of the working end is next to the first stitch of the starting end. (Fig. 6)

Fig. 6

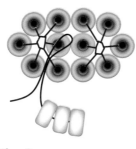

3. Tape the two ends together in this position so the beads assume a shape. (Fig. 7) Thread the required number of beads onto a new thread; pull up a loop through one of the outer stitches as shown. Crochet around the 10 outer beads. You will notice

Fig. 7

Fig. 8

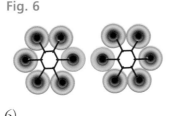

that the beads of the starting end are already positioned horizontally; it may take a bit of force to push the hook through and pass the bead to the far side of the hook. (Fig. 8)

The beads of the finishing end will be positioned correctly and no force will be necessary.

4. Work a second round of 10 beads. Decrease two stitches in the next round by slip-stitching without a bead in the beads (green). (Fig. 9)

Fig. 9

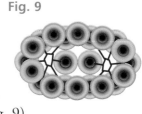

5. Work another round in which you skip the stitches that have only a slip stitch and no bead. The two beads on either side of the slip stitch will be drawn together. Work another round of eight. (Fig. 10)

Fig. 10

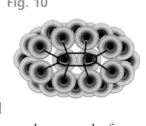

6. Work a slip stitch without a bead in the next round in the beads (green). (Fig. 11) Work another round in which you skip the slip stitches without beads. The two beads on either side of the slip stitch will be drawn together. (Fig. 12)

Fig. 11

Fig. 12

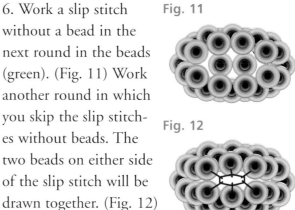

7. Work as many additional rounds of six as desired. When you are satisfied with the length, crochet one round of slip stitch only, without beads. This will cause the beads of the last round to lie horizontally, as the beads of all the completed rounds lie.

Joining Three Tube Ends to Reduce to One

1. Complete the tube crochet so each of the three tubes is the desired length. For each tube, bind off the last stitch of the working end, then bury starting and ending thread tails within the fibers of their tube.

2. Position the three ends together so the last stitch of each tube (shown in green) is on the inside of the assembly. (Fig. 13) Tape the tubes together. (Fig. 14)

Fig. 13

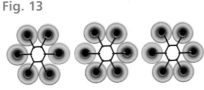

Fig. 14

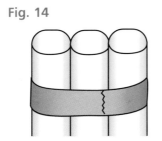

3. Pull up a new thread. (Fig. 15) Crochet all around the taped tubes, working only in the beads shown in light yellow.

Fig. 15

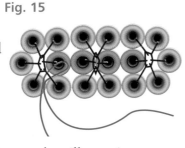

The beads shown in purple will remain uncrocheted and will recede into the center of the new 14-bead tube.

4. A single tube will be established with the new round crocheted. (Fig. 16) Add one round of 14 beads.

Fig. 16

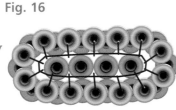

5. In the next round, slip-stitch without a bead in the beads shown in green. (Fig. 17) Add one more round, but skip over the slip stitches without beads, thereby reducing the number of beads in the round to 12. (Fig. 18)

Fig. 17

Fig. 18

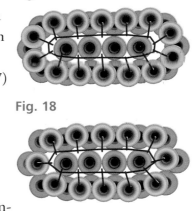

6. Slip-stitch without a bead in the beads shown in green in the next round. (Fig. 19) In the next round after that, skip over the slip stitches, thereby reducing the number of beads in the new round to 10.

Fig. 19

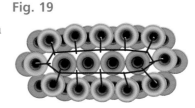

7. Continue in this manner, reducing by one bead at each end in every other round. Slip-stitch the beads shown in green when you have 10 beads in the round. (Fig. 20)

Fig. 20

Fig. 21

Continue until there are only six beads in the round. (Fig. 21) Continue to any desired length.

8. When you are satisfied with the length, crochet one round of slip stitch only, without beads. This will cause the beads of the last round to lie horizontally, as the beads of all the completed rounds lie.

Surrounding a Cabochon

Cabochons—flat-backed stones or glass shapes without holes—can be set in tubular crochet. Since cabochons vary in size, shape, and depth, there are no precise directions for encasing them. The possibilities for design fun are multiplied exponentially by the tremendous variety in the size and shape of the seed beads used for the surrounding tube.

The basic concept is to combine beaded crochet and peyote stitch, which mimic each other in appearance. One might reasonably ask why a beader would choose to use beaded crochet to surround a cabochon instead of tubular peyote. The answer is flexibility. A long beaded crochet rope can be tied in knots while tubular peyote can be quite stiff depending on the type and size of beads and the stitch tension of the beader. You can pick up every other bead along the side edge of a crocheted tube and pretend that you are working on an established piece of peyote stitch. By adding more beads on the established "ridge" in the peyote stitch manner, you can build out a strip of beadwork that will hold a cabochon in place.

There are two methods for enclosing a cabochon in beaded crochet. In the first method, the tube will be fitted around the outside edge of the cabochon such as in the Lemon Blossom

Necklace on pages 102–104. In the second method, the the crocheted tube is fitted around the edge of the cabochon, but fitted so it just skirts the inside of the piece such as in the Looking Glass Necklace

Fig. 22

on pages 108–110. In this case, the tube itself has a lot of design importance, because more of the cabochon will be covered. In either method, you will need to create a tube of crochet that has an even number of rounds. Because adjustability is critical, the choice of patterns is somewhat limited to those that have a low even number of rounds in each repeat. One-color tubes or alternating spirals are best. (Fig. 22) These are easily adjusted for fit around the cabochon because you can add or remove rows so the fit is correct and the pattern lines up properly.

Note: If you plan to add a "bail" of beads that will cover the joint, you can use a pattern that does not align. The alignment is critical only if the joint will be visible.

1. Complete the crocheted tube but do not cut the thread or remove excess beads from the thread—you may need them for small adjustments. The tube should fit precisely around the cabochon—snug against the outer edge.

2. Thread a #10 needle with a coordinating color of nylon beading thread; make a small knot at one end. Bring the new thread out in any bead in the first or second round of the

Fig. 23

Fig. 24

tube. Pick up one 11o seed bead, skip one round on the tube, then insert the needle into a bead in the next round that is in the same position on the round as the previous bead (beads shown in green). (Fig. 23) Continue in this manner, skipping beads and adding beads until the initial ridge runs the entire length of the tube. You will notice that this process mimics peyote stitch. When you come to the end of the tube, line up the ends of the tube so the added row lines up to itself. (Fig. 24) There should be one bead left at the end of the tube.

3. Set aside the stitching thread. Examine the ends of the tube to see if they line up properly to create an invisible join with the added row in alignment to itself. If necessary, add or remove crochet stitches so the alignment is correct. When the fit is right, bind off the last stitch. Refer to Making an Invisible Join on pages 20–21. Join the ends invisibly and bury excess thread within the tube.

4. Pick up the thread again in the first bead of the ridge row. At this point, you will begin the second ridge row. Continue around until the second ridge row is complete (beads shown in purple). (Fig. 25)

Fig. 25

5. Refer to Peyote Stitch on pages 26–27. Work in peyote stitch until your strip is sufficient to hold the cabochon. The peyote strip will decrease in circumference as you add rows; this is accomplished by changing bead size and decreasing beads in the final rows. (Fig. 26) You must start the peyote stitch using the same size bead as was used in the tube, but as you add rows, you can use smaller beads. For example, in the Lemon Blossom Necklace, the surrounding tube is worked in 11o seed beads. The first two rounds of peyote are worked in beads of the same size. The third and fourth rounds, however, are worked in delica beads, which are slightly smaller than 11o seed beads. The fifth and sixth rows are worked in 15o seed beads, which are slightly smaller than delica beads. Thereafter, the work is completed in 15o seed beads, but

Fig. 26

each round is decreased by a few beads by passing over a natural bead placement and advancing to the next placement space. Bury the thread in the work.

Note: Use your own best judgement as to how many times in each round you should pass over a placement space—often it is a matter of trial and error.

6. When you have completed the work on the front, position the cabochon in the surround and turn it over to begin work on the back. (Fig. 27) Use a non-residue tape, such as masking tape, to secure the cabochon in position. As was done for

Fig. 27

Fig. 28

the front, bring a new thread out from within the tube. Add the first round of peyote using the same size bead as was used in the tube. Work peyote stitch to enclose the cabochon, reducing as needed and adding enough rows to ensure that the cabochon will not slip out. (Fig. 28)

Fig. 29

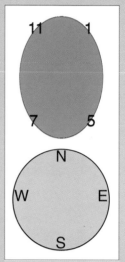

Note: Because the back of the cabochon is flat and the front perhaps more domed, you will decrease more quickly so the peyote will sit flat against the back of the cabochon. You may want to switch to a smaller size of bead in the second round of peyote. Generally, the decreasing positions for rounded cabochons will be at the points of the compass (N, S, E, W). On oval cabochons, the back decreases can be made in the clock positions of 11, 1, 5, and 7 in the first round of decreases. (Fig. 29) In the second round, try making the decreases at the compass positions.

Peyote Stitch

Peyote stitch is a non-loomed bead-weaving technique. Seed beads, delica beads, and hex beads are widely used with this method. Choose needles and thread that work with the type of bead you are using. Short ballpoint beading needles in #10 or #12 are a better choice than longer beading needles.

The peyote stitch creates staggered rows of beads that lie vertically against one another and yield a diagonal effect when the entire design is woven.

1. Complete the ridge row and join the tube ends. Add the next round of beads in peyote stitch. (Fig. 30 on page 27)

Fig. 30

2. Hitch up the next round. (Fig. 31)

Fig. 31

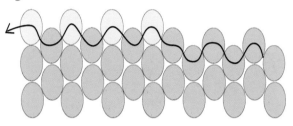

3. Following the path of the thread as shown, add the beads of Row 3. (Fig. 32)

Fig. 32

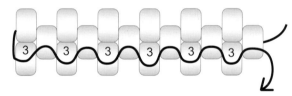

4. Add Row 4 in the same manner as Row 3. (Fig. 33) Continue to achieve desired length.

Fig. 33

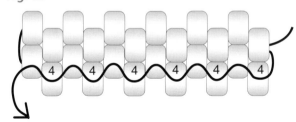

5. Reduce beads in the round as needed. (Fig. 34)

Fig. 34

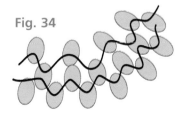

Brick Stitch

Brick stitch is a non-loom-weaving technique that creates a strong diagonal weave similar to peyote stitch. However, the brick stitch causes beads to lie against one another horizontally. Designs are worked in horizontal rows and may be shaped by increasing or decreasing.

Note: The diagrams shown here are exaggerated for clarity. When working brick stitch, keep the tension even and consistent; take up the slack in the thread after adding each bead. Avoid pulling too tightly, or the weave may pucker.

1. Begin working brick stitch by creating a foundation row consisting of beads joined side to side with thread. You can use either the double-needle technique (Fig. 35) or the single-needle technique (Fig. 36). In the single-needle method, turn the foundation row so the thread emerges from the bottom of the bead in preparation for starting the second row.

Fig. 35

Fig. 36

2. After working the double-needle foundation row, let one thread lie dormant while you work rows with the other. Beads are applied individually, looped into the thread between beads on the previous row. Work rows back and forth as charted, increasing or decreasing as required. The top edge of the piece will appear smooth, while the side edges will appear jagged.

Symmetrical brick stitch is often used for flat or stand-alone designs. Notice that the number of beads in each row will alternate plus or minus one bead. Work the pattern from the foundation row to the bottom. (Fig. 37)

Fig. 37

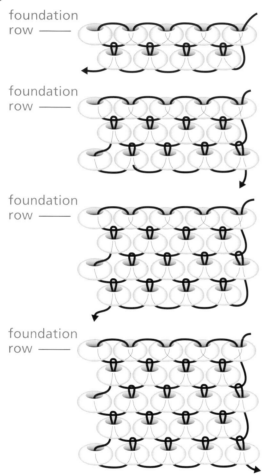

foundation row

foundation row

foundation row

foundation row

Increases are made at the beginning and end of each row. The basic concept in increasing is to add beads in the same manner as the single-needle foundation row. When increasing on the right side, work the thread back through the added beads until it emerges from the bottom

of the first bead added, then proceed through the rest of the row. (Fig. 38)

Fig. 38

increase on the right

Add beads on the left in a similar manner, again making certain that the thread emerges from the bottom of the last bead in the row. (Fig. 39)

Fig. 39

increase on the left

Decreases on the right are made by working the thread back through beads on the end of the row until the thread emerges in proper position to continue as charted. (Fig. 40)

Fig. 40

decrease on the right

To decrease on the left, simply end the row in the indicated position and bring the thread out of the bottom of the last bead, so the next row can be started. (Fig. 41)

Fig. 41

decrease on the left

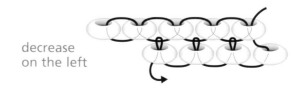

blank patterns

Use these blank pattern overview and detail diagrams to create your own six-around, seven-around, and eight-around beaded crochet designs.

Six-around Pattern Diagrams

Seven-around Pattern Diagrams

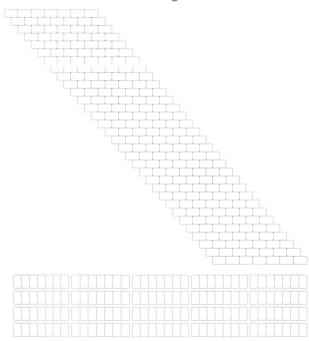

Eight-around Pattern Diagrams

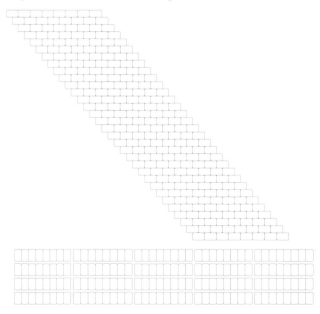

I feel pretty

little mermaid necklace

Materials

2.5mm seed pearls, 16" strands (5)

10mm round pearls (2)

14mm stick pearl

14mm–20mm central drop pearl, side-drilled

Ivory nylon beading thread, medium-weight

28-gauge gold beading wire (5")

#12 steel crochet hook

Instructions

Note: Four and one-half strands were required to create the 16" necklace.

1. Thread on enough beads to create a necklace of the desired length. You will use 60 per inch of rope.

2. Crochet in six-around tube. Finish the working end with one round of unbeaded slip stitch.

3. Add the toggle and loop. (Fig. 1) If possible, reinforce with a second pass of thread, if it will fit through the pearls.

4. Wrap and secure the central pearl drop to the rope with gold wire. (Fig. 2)

Fig. 1

Fig. 2

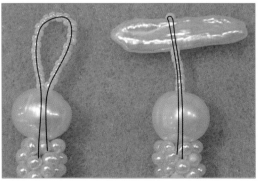

34 simple tube patterns

blue jeans set

The bangle featured here is a good example of how fiber and beads can interplay to create a wonderful effect. The beads used in this bracelet are actually transparent light blue; however, when used over the dark navy cotton, they take on a muted denim-like tone.

Bangle Materials

- 80 seed beads, Toho #13F, matte transparent light sapphire (10 grams)
- 80 seed beads, Czech, silk-finish silver (3 grams)
- 7mm x 10mm faceted rondelle, denim lapis

- 10mm silver bead caps (2)
- Silver beading wire, lightweight flexible
- #8 or #10 dark navy perle cotton

- #10 steel crochet hook

Bangle Instructions

1. Refer to Counting from Patterns on page 17. Following Blue Jeans Pattern Detail, thread on enough repeats to equal the measurement of the wrist size minus ½". (For a 6½" bracelet, approximately 40 repeats of the pattern are required.)

2. Crochet a six-around tube; bind off and bury both tails within the fibers of the tube.

3. Refer to Finishing with a Focal Bead on pages 21–22. Add the bead caps and lapis bead.

Blue Jeans Pattern Detail

Blue Jeans Pattern Overview

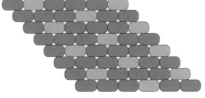

Earring Materials

2.5mm silver beads (4)

3mm x 10mm Czech glass spears, frosted light sapphire (60)

5mm round sterling spacers (4)

8mm round faceted fresh-water pearls, blue (4)

12mm round faceted freshwater pearls, blue (2)

Ear wires, sterling silver (2)

2½" 24-gauge head pins, sterling silver (2)

Topstitching thread, light blue

#10 steel crochet hook

Earring Instructions

1. Thread on 30 glass spears.

2. Crochet in six-around tube until all the beads are used.

3. Bury the excess tails within the fibers of the tube.

4. Stack beads on the head pin, from bottom to top, as follows: 2.5mm silver bead, 8mm pearl, two silver spacers, 12mm pearl, tube of crochet, 8mm pearl, and 2.5mm silver bead.

5. Cut the head pin to ⅜" excess. Form a loop using round-nosed pliers and close the loop on the ear wire.

6. Repeat Steps 1–5 for second earring.

moonbeam bracelet

This bracelet uses Matsuno beads, which have a shape and size that is peculiar to that type of bead alone. They are actually more like #1 bugles in size and finish. As the bracelet moves, the satin beads give off a wonderful little flash.

Materials

11o seed beads, Matsuno #365, satin aqua (3 per round)

11o seed beads, Matsuno #367, satin eggshell, (3 per round)

10mm x 14mm focal bead, aqua

8mm gold bead caps (2)

Eggshell topstitching thread

#10 steel crochet hook

Instructions

1. Create the pattern by alternating bead colors. Thread on beads to equal a 45" length.

2. Crochet in six-around tube to create a bracelet of approximately 6" length.

3. Refer to Finishing with a Focal Bead on pages 21–22. Join the two ends of the bracelet together at the focal bead.

china doll necklace

Materials

11o seed beads, any one color (50 grams)

Finishing beads, as desired

8mm gold bead caps (2)

Coordinating topstitching thread

Gold clasp

Knot Diagram

⭐ = points at which knot is secured with invisible stitches

Instructions

Note: This necklace is created with a six-around tube worked in one color of 11o seed beads with topstitching thread.

1. Before beginning determine how long you would like the necklace to be, then add 10" of rope—that is the amount needed to form the knot itself. Thread on enough beads to equal the desired length.

2. Crochet a six-around tube until all beads are crocheted.

3. Following Knot Diagram, work the knot so it lands in the center of the length.

4. Secure the knot with invisible stitches at the star points indicated on the diagram.

5. Add finishing beads as desired; use lightweight nylon to sew them in place.

6. Add bead caps and clasp to finish the ends of the necklace.

sugarplum bracelet

Materials

- 8o seed beads, Czech #57100, silver-lined light green (6 per repeat)
- 8o seed beads, Czech #97101, silver-lined red (2 per repeat)
- 8o seed beads, Czech #58135, transparent crystal AB (10 per repeat)
- 6mm fire-polish faceted beads, red (2)
- 6mm square beads, gold (2)
- 6mm x 8mm abacus faceted freshwater pearls, dyed green (4)
- 8mm x 11mm ovals, malachite (2)

#10 white perle cotton
10mm gold bead caps (2)
Clear glue
Memory wire (1½ loops)

#10 steel crochet hook
Round-nosed pliers
Wire cutters, heavy-weight

Instructions

1. Refer to Counting from Patterns on page 17. Following Sugarplum Pattern Detail, thread on enough repeats to create a 48" length.

Sugarplum Pattern Detail

Sugarplum Pattern Overview

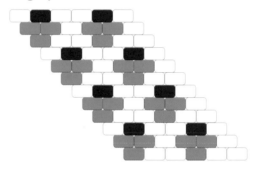

2. Crochet in six-around tube until tube measures 1" less than the wrist.

3. Bind off and bury the starting and ending tails within the fiber of the tube.

4. If necessary, cut the end of the memory wire to remove any burrs. Carefully run the memory wire through the center of the tube so wire protrudes from both ends. Tape one end with masking tape while you are working on the other end.

Note: It may take patience and persistence to thread the memory wire through the tube. Work the wire forward and backward in short bursts.

5. Refer to photo. Thread the cap and remaining beads for one side of the bracelet.

6. Following End Bead Diagram and using pliers, make a slight bend in the last ⅜" of the memory wire. Dip the end of the wire in glue and insert the wire into the malachite until the end of the wire is flush with the end of the bead. Push the tube and beads so they are next to malachite. Allow the assembly to dry.

End Bead Diagram

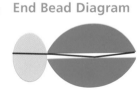

7. Thread on the cap and beads for the remaining side, including the malachite. Cut the end of the wire flush with the end of the malachite, remove the malachite, and make another slight bend. Dip the wire in glue and reposition the malachite. Allow to dry.

snow queen necklace

Materials

8o seed beads, Miyuki #131, crystal AB (60 per inch of rope)

5mm x 9mm rectangular glass beads (2)

8mm round beads, silver (2)

Suspended leaf bead, silver (2)

Large central mother-of-pearl piece, silver-wrapped with side loops visible

10mm silver bead caps (4)

22-gauge silver beading wire (8")

Light blue rayon or silk fiber, crochet-weight

#10 steel crochet hook

Instructions

1. Slide 8o seed beads onto fiber to create a rope approximately 10" long. Crochet and bind off. Repeat for a second rope.

2. Finish rope ends, using the tails to pull in the beads of the last round.

3. Finish the clasp ends.

4. Cut two 2½" pieces of wire. Make a hook in one end of each piece and snag it within the tube end. Following Necklace Assembly Diagram, add the cap and beads, then cut the wire to ⅜" excess. Make a loop in the excess and hook it through the side loops on the central pendant. Close the loop securely.

Necklace Assembly Diagram

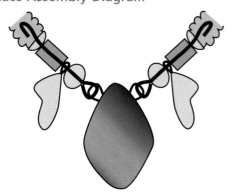

springtime earrings

Materials

 15o seed beads, Miyuki #2033, matte metallic green (2 grams)

15o seed beads, Miyuki #3, silver-lined light gold (1 gram)

2.5mm round beads, gold (8)

5mm bicone crystals, topaz (6)

10mm x 14mm freshwater pearls, olive (2)

7mm gold bead caps (4)

24-gauge gold beading wire (8")

Gold ear wires open-ended (2)

1¼" 24-gauge gold head pins (2)

7mm gold split rings (2)

Ochre topstitching thread

#13 steel crochet hook

Round-nosed pliers

Wire cutters

Instructions

1. Following Drop Diagram, stack the beads on the head pin to create the center drop. Trim the excess head pin to ⅜" and form a loop at the end.

2. Refer to Counting from Patterns on page 17. Following Springtime Pattern Detail, thread on 14 repeats. End by adding six matte metallic olive 15o seed beads.

3. Crochet tube; bind off and bury the tails at both ends. Take care not to fill the center of the tube with thread.

Drop Diagram

Springtime Pattern Detail

Springtime Pattern Overview

4. Cut the wire into two equal pieces. Remove any burrs on the tips of the wires. Run one wire length through tube. Center the crochet tube on the wire length.

5. Add the caps and beads to the sides of the wired tube. Using pliers, make a wrapped loop ⅛" in diameter at one end of the wire and move the beads close together until they touch the loop. Without trimming, make another loop at the remaining side of the wire so the wrapped loop keeps the beads close to each other.

6. Open the split ring and join both wrapped loops onto the split ring.

7. Following Earring Assembly Diagram, add the center drop onto the split ring between the two wrapped loops. Place the entire assembly onto the ear wire's loop.

8. Repeat Steps 1–7 for second earring.

Earring Assembly Diagram

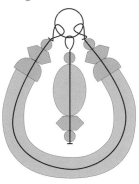

tiger lily necklace

This is another good example of how a transparent bead and a colored or textured fiber can interact beautifully. The overall essence of this necklace is turquoise, yet the beads themselves are transparent brass-lined with an aurora borealis finish. It's the fiber that shows through, lending its character to the overall appearance of the necklace.

Materials

- 80 seed beads, Czech #68506, brass-lined crystal AB (60 per inch of rope)
- 4mm vermeil decorative spacers (2)
- 6mm cut crystals, dark topaz (2)
- 6mm vermeil spacers (2)
- 8mm cut crystals, dark topaz (2)
- Large central turquoise drop, briolette-shaped, top-drilled
- 10mm vermeil bead caps for clasp end (2)
- 22-gauge gold beading wire (12")
- Small vermeil bead caps for crystals (4)
- Vermeil S-hook clasp
- Turquoise rayon or silk fiber, crochet-weight
- #10 steel crochet hook
- Round-nosed pliers
- Wire cutters

Instructions

Note: All of the beads in the crocheted rope are the same color.

1. Thread on enough beads to create a necklace of the desired length.

2. Crochet in six-around tube. Bind off the last stitch. Using the tails to finish each end of the rope, run the needle through the last round of beads and pull the thread so the beads close in to create a rounded end. (Figs. 1–2)

Fig. 1

Fig. 2

Thank heaven for little girls.

3. Following Center Assembly Diagram, assemble the center. Slide the beads onto the wire, leaving an excess of ¾" at one end. Bend the ¾" section into a loop (bend at either side of the turquoise drop), then cut the remaining end of the wire so an excess of ¾" is left. Bend that ¾" section into a loop to complete the center.

Center Assembly Diagram

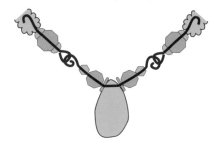

4. Cut two 2½" pieces of wire. Make a small hook in one end and snag the hook within the fibers of the rope. Add one small cap, one large crystal, and one small cap on the protruding wire, then cut it to ⅜". Make a closed loop in the excess; hook the curl on the center drop into the closed loop.

5. Add bead caps and clasp to finish the ends of the necklace.

butterfly kisses bracelet

Materials
8o seed beads, Czech #58135, transparent crystal AB (60 per inch of rope)

#10 variegated blue perle cotton

#10 steel crochet hook

Instructions
1. Thread on enough repeats to create a 48" length.

2. Crochet in six-around tube until the tube is slightly larger than the wrist.

3. Bind off, leaving a 10" tail.

4. Bury the starting tail within the fibers of the tube. Refer to Making an Invisible Join on pages 20–21. Use the ending tail to join the two ends invisibly.

5. Bury the excess ending tail within the fibers of the tube and clip close.

polka-dots bangle

Materials

- 80 seed beads, Czech #30050 or Toho #8, transparent dark sapphire (9 per repeat)
- 80 seed beads, Toho #161 or Miyuki #131F, transparent matte crystal (3 per repeat)
- 10mm "dotted" glass bead, blue/white
- #10 navy blue perle cotton
- #10 steel crochet hook

Instructions

1. Refer to Counting from Patterns on page 17. Following Polka-dots Pattern Detail, thread on enough repeats to equal the circumference of the wrist.

2. Crochet in a six-around tube.

3. Work one more round of unbeaded slip stitch.

4. Refer to Finishing with a Focal Bead on pages 21–22. Join the two ends of the bracelet together at the dotted bead.

Polka-dots Pattern Detail

Polka-dots Pattern Overview

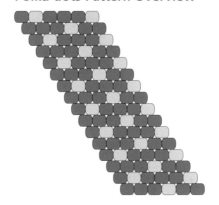

sweetheart bracelet

Materials

- 11o seed beads, matte transparent purple (14 per repeat)
- 11o seed beads, opaque light blue (6 per repeat)
- 11o seed beads, opaque yellow (16 per repeat)
- 10mm x 18mm focal bead with heart pattern

- 8mm gold bead caps (2)
- Medium purple topstitching thread

- #11 steel crochet hook

Instructions

1. Refer to Counting from Patterns on page 17. Following Sweetheart Pattern Detail, thread on enough repeats to create a 50" length.

2. Crochet in six-around tube until tube measures ½" less than the wrist.

3. Bind off and bury the starting tail within the fibers of the tube.

4. Refer to Finishing with a Focal Bead on pages 21–22. Finish with the heart-patterned bead in the center.

Sweetheart Pattern Detail

Sweetheart Pattern Overview

Alternate Eight-around Pattern Overview

my favorite things

56 different sized beads

different sized beads

pixie-pink necklace

This necklace can be made in literally any color, since the perceived color of the beads is actually determined by the thread—the beads are clear with an aurora borealis finish. In this case, the interior thread is persimmon, but it could just as easily have been any other color of rayon. The pattern can be worked using cotton, but the rayon has a lustrous finish that enhances the sparkle of the fire-polish beads. Silk might be substituted nicely.

Materials

11o seed beads, Miyuki #250 or Toho #161 or Czech #58195, crystal AB (5 grams)

3mm fire-polish beads, crystal AB (140)

4mm fire-polish beads, crystal AB (140)

6mm fire-polish beads, crystal AB (70)

8mm x 14mm cut crystals, crystal AB (2)

15mm flat bead with center hole

Persimmon rayon thread

Transparent nylon beading thread, lightweight

#10 beading needle

#10 steel crochet hook

Instructions

1. Following Pixie-pink Necklace Threading Pattern, thread 14 repeats onto rayon thread, then add another thirty-five 11o beads. This will yield a 16" necklace. For a longer or shorter necklace, adjust the pattern accordingly.

Pixie-pink Necklace Threading Pattern

35 □ 5 ○ 5 ⬡ 5 ⯃ 5 ⬡ 5 ○

2. Crochet in a five-around tube; bind off.

3. Place a needle on the ending tail and draw in the threads of the last round by running the tail thread through all of them and pulling them in. Bury the tail threads of both ends within the tube.

4. Thread nylon beading thread in beading needle and secure it within either end of the tube. Bring the thread out in the center of the last round of beads. Following the Loop Diagram, add beads to one end. Following the Toggle Diagram, add beads to the remaining end. Reinforce both the loop and the center-hole bead with a second pass of thread, then secure the thread within the fibers of the tube. Clip close.

Loop Diagram   **Toggle Diagram**

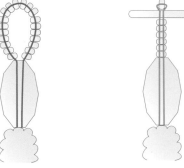

Which way to Hollywood?

58 different sized beads

poppy bangle

Materials

- 11o seed beads, Toho #162B, transparent topaz (9 per repeat)
- 8o seed beads, Toho #45 or Czech #93210, opaque red (3 per repeat)

#10 white perle cotton

#10 steel crochet hook

Instructions

1. Refer to Counting from Patterns on page 17. Following Poppy Pattern Detail, thread on enough repeats to create a 48" length.

2. Crochet in six-around tube until the tube is slightly larger than the wrist, ending with a full repeat.

3. Bind off, leaving a 10" tail.

4. Bury the starting tail within the fibers of the tube. Refer to Making an Invisible Join on pages 20–21. Use the ending tail to join two ends invisibly.

5. Bury the excess ending tail within the fibers of the tube and clip close.

Poppy Pattern Detail

Poppy Pattern Overview

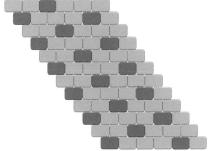

60 different sized beads

treasure box set

This set features an elegant necklace that is created using 8o seed beads, 6o seed beads, and #5 triangle beads. The center slide is worked with delicas in brick stitch and is embellished with pearls. At the base of the center slide, a large handmade glass bead is suspended.

Necklace Materials

- Delica beads, #324, matte metallic green (3 grams)
- Delica beads, #42, silver-lined light amber (3 grams)
- 8o seed beads, Czech #10070, transparent amber (24 per inch of rope)
- 6o seed beads, Czech #17020, silver-lined amber (24 per inch of rope)
- #5 triangle beads, Miyuki #1165, green-lined light amber (12 per inch of rope)
- 6mm fire-polish crystal, olive
- 8mm button pearl, bronze (2)

Large central drop bead to suspend from the slider

#8 topaz perle cotton (25 yards)
10mm gold bead caps (2)
Dark green nylon beading thread, heavy-weight
Gold clasp

#10 steel crochet hook
Round-nosed pliers
Wire cutters

Necklace Instructions

1. Slide twelve 8o seed beads onto perle cotton . Refer to Counting from Patterns on page 17. Following Treasure Box Pattern Detail, slide on beads until there are enough repeats to desired length; end with twenty-four 8o seed beads. Two repeats of the pattern equal approximately 1".

Treasure Box Pattern Overview

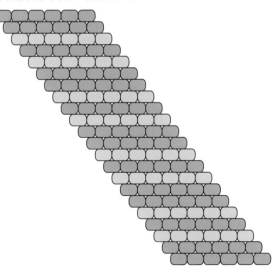

Treasure Box Pattern Detail

2. Crochet rope; bind off.

3. Refer to Brick Stitch on pages 27–28. Using brick stitch and following Slider Pattern, create the slider and suspend the center drop beads.

4. Following Embellishment Diagrams, add the pearls, 6mm fire-polish crystal, and bead embellishments as indicated.

5. Fold slider in half and join together at the "Vs".

6. Slip the slider onto the rope. Add the caps and clasp.

Slider Pattern

Embellishment Diagrams

Top view

Side view

Earring Assembly Diagram

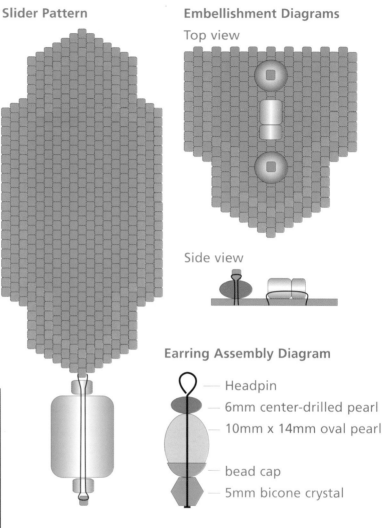

— Headpin
— 6mm center-drilled pearl
— 10mm x 14mm oval pearl

— bead cap
— 5mm bicone crystal

Earring Materials
5mm bicone crystals, metallic green (2)
6mm center-drilled pearl, bronze (2)
10mm x 14mm oval pearl (2)

10mm gold bead caps (2)
2" 24-gauge gold head pins (2)

Needle-nosed pliers
Wire cutters

62 different sized beads

Earring Instructions
1. Following the Earring Assembly Diagram, stack the beads on the head pin.

2. Cut the head pin so there is an excess of ⅜".

3. Using round-nosed pliers, turn a loop in the excess to form a question mark. Slip the loop on the ear wire and close the loop with the pliers.

stardust bracelet

stardust bracelet

Materials

8o seed beads, Toho #557F, matte metallic gold (60 per inch of rope)

4mm fire-polish crystals, gold-finish (20 per inch of rope)

13mm x 18mm focal bead

10mm gold bead caps (2)

#8 topaz perle cotton

#10 steel crochet hook

Instructions

1. Thread eighteen 8o seed beads onto perle cotton. Refer to Counting from Patterns on page 17. Following Stardust Pattern Detail, thread on 22 repeats or desired inches of rope; end with twenty-one 8o seed beads.

Note: Seed beads are used at the beginning and end of this pattern so the bead caps will fit well; crystals lying under the caps will place the cap out of position.

2. Crochet a six-around tube; bind off and bury both tails within the fibers of the tube.

3. Refer to Finishing with a Focal Bead on pages 21–22. Add the bead caps and focal bead.

Stardust Pattern Detail

Stardust Pattern Overview

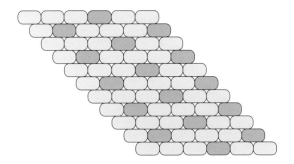

Stardust Bracelet Variation

Make a completely original bracelet using this pattern by simply substituting different beads.

Notes: You may notice that the seed beads in this pattern don't line up as neatly as they do in patterns where all the beads are the same size. This happens because of the odd shape of the 4mm fire-polish. They tend to muscle the seed beads out of position, but over the entire bracelet, the mispositioning will be consistent, which creates a rather pleasing out-of-kilter effect.

One thing to watch for in this pattern is the tendency to drop a stitch. Take care to check every couple of rounds that you are still in pattern by looking at the side of the tube and counting the beads in the top round.

You otta be in pictures!

black beauty set

Necklace Materials

- 15o seed beads, Toho #610 or Miyuki #401F, matte black (1 gram)
- Delicas, Miyuki #401F, matte black (12)
- 11o seed beads, Toho #610 or Miyuki #401F, matte black (12)
- 11o seed beads, Toho #558F, matte silver (4 grams)
- 8o hex-cut beads, Toho #610, matte black (1 gram)
- 3.3mm cylinder beads, Toho #620, matte black (12)
- Tiny raindrop beads, Czech, opaque black (18)
- Japanese drop beads, Miyuki #401, opaque black (36)
- 5mm drop beads, Czech, opaque black (24)
- 6mm fire-polish beads, Czech, matte black (16)
- 6mm rondelles, Czech, opaque black (2)
- 8mm rondelles, Czech, opaque black (4)
- 9mm x 18mm teardrops, Czech, opaque black (2)
- 15mm crescent bead for toggle, half-silver

Dark gray topstitching thread

#10 steel crochet hook

Necklace Instructions

1. Slide beads onto the fiber in this order: *Twelve 15o seed beads; six delicas, six black 11o seed beads, six 8o hex beads, six 3.3mm cylinder beads, six tiny raindrop beads, six 5mm drop beads, six Japanese drop beads; nine silver 11o seed beads, one tiny raindrop bead, [three silver 11o seed beads, one tiny raindrop eight times], nine silver 11o seed beads, six Japanese drop beads, six 5mm drop beads*; six 6mm fire-polish matte black. Repeat between *s in reverse order.

2. Leave a 15" thread tail before making the starting slip knot. This tail will later be used in constructing the necklace strand.

3. Work in a six-around tube until all the beads have been used. Leave an 18" thread tail at the end after binding off.

4. Place a needle on each of the two long thread tails and run the thread into the crochet tube, then out again so the thread is centered in the end of the tube.

5. Following Necklace Assembly Diagram on page 68, slide on beads until each side of the necklace is the desired length.

6. Add the crescent toggle at one end and make a loop of 15o black seed beads at the remaining end.

7. Run both threads back through their respective strands and bury the strands within the crocheted tube. Trim off excess.

Earring Materials
11o seed beads, Toho #558F, matte silver (24)
6mm fire-polish beads, Czech, matte black (2)
9mm x 18mm teardrops, Czech, opaque black (2)

Silver ear wires (2)
Dark gray topstitching thread

Earring Instructions

Earring Assembly Diagram

1. Following Earring Assembly Diagram, thread on the beads. Take all the slack out of the thread. Tie a knot so it lands within the large teardrop. Trim excess thread.

2. Open the top loop of 11o beads and slip in the loop from the ear wire. Close the loop on the ear wire.

68 different sized beads

Necklace Assembly Diagram

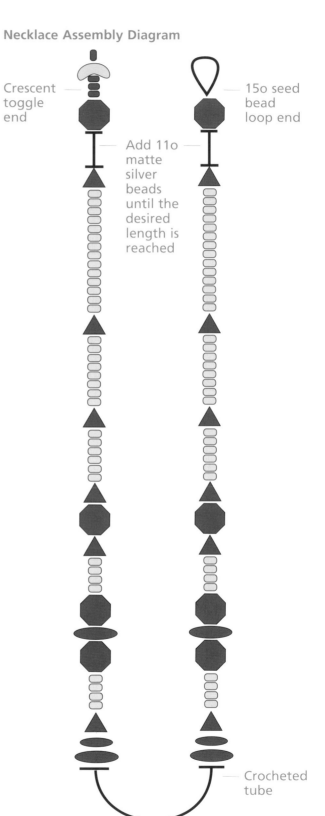

Crescent toggle end

15o seed bead loop end

Add 11o matte silver beads until the desired length is reached

Crocheted tube

pretty in pink set

pretty in pink set

Necklace Materials

15o seed beads, Miyuki #26, pink (30)

3mm fire-polish crystals, crystal AB (40 per inch of rope)

7mm–8mm cut crystals, deep pink (3)

8mm–9mm cut crystal, deep pink (1)

14mm round handmade glass bead, pink (1)

15mm stick pearls, center-drilled, rose (2)

25mm stick pearls, center-drilled, rose (2)

2" silver head pin with fancy crystal end

Transparent nylon beading thread, lightweight

#8 or #10 deep rose pink perle cotton (30 yards)

#10 beading needle

#10 steel crochet hook

Round-nosed pliers

Wire cutters

Necklace Instructions

1. Thread forty 3mm fire-polish crystals per inch onto perle cotton to desired necklace length. The necklace shown is 16" of rope length, using 640 beads.

2. Crochet in a five-around tube until the length is achieved. Cut the perle cotton and bind off. Bury both tails within the fibers of the tube.

3. Thread nylon beading thread onto beading needle and secure it invisibly within either end of the tube. Bring the thread out in the center of the last round of beads. Following the Loop Diagram, add beads to one end. Following the Toggle Diagram, add beads to the remaining end. Reinforce both the loop and the center-hole bead on the toggle with a second pass of thread, then secure the thread within the fibers of the tube. Clip closely.

Loop Diagram

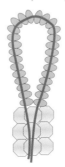

Toggle Diagram

Earring Materials

5mm cut crystals, deep pink (2)

7mm–8mm cut crystals, deep pink (2)

8mm x 10mm handmade glass beads, pink (2)

15mm stick pearls, center-drilled, rose (2)

Silver ear wires (2)

2" silver head pins with fancy crystal end (2)

Round-nosed pliers

Wire cutters

Earring Instructions

1. Following the Assembly Diagram, stack the beads, then form a small loop at the top of the head pin just above the last bead.

2. Wrap the wire around the loop to secure it, then clip off the excess, using wire cutters.

3. Open the bottom loop of each ear wire and join the assembly onto the ear wire. Using pliers, close the ear wire loop securely.

Assembly Diagram

4. Following the Drop Diagram, stack the beads onto the head pin for the center drop. Make a large wrapped loop in the end of the head pin; make certain the head pin loop is large enough to slip over the beaded loop at the end of the necklace strand.

5. Center the drop on the necklace rope.

Drop Diagram

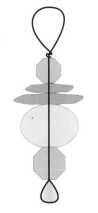

island princess bracelet

Materials

- 11o seed beads, Toho #560F, matte galvanized light green (39 per repeat)

- 11o seed beads, Miyuki #2020 or Toho #707, matte metallic green AB (22 per repeat)

- 8o seed beads, Toho #24BF, matte silver-lined medium green (18 per repeat)

- Magatama beads, matte transparent light green (6 per repeat)

- 3mm x 10mm glass spears, Czech, matte transparent light green (6 per repeat)

- 3mm x 10mm glass spears, Czech, matte transparent light pink (6 per repeat)

- 3mm x 5mm glass drop beads, Czech, opal pink (6 per repeat)

- 4mm fire-polish faceted glass beads, crystal AB (6 per repeat)

#10 light green perle cotton

#10 steel crochet hook

Instructions

1. Following Island Princess Threading Pattern, starting with the top row and threading the pattern from left to right, slide beads onto thread. Repeat four times to create a 6¼" bracelet.

2. Crochet in six-around tube until all the beads are used.

3. Bury the beginning tail. Refer to Making an Invisible Join on pages 20–21. Use the ending tail to make an invisible join.

Island Princess Threading Pattern

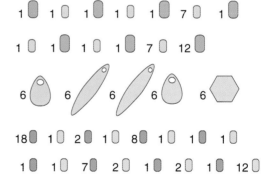

1 1 1 1 1 7 1

1 1 1 1 7 12

6 6 6 6 6

18 1 2 1 8 1 1 1

1 1 7 2 1 2 1 12

All dressed up with no place to go.

island princess bracelet **73**

it's all about accessories

complex tube patterns

snake charmer set

Bracelet Materials

11o seed beads, Czech #63130M, opaque matte green turquoise (2 grams)

11o seed beads, Czech #03152, opaque pale green (6 grams)

11o seed beads, Czech #59195, purple iris (1 gram)

11o seed beads, Czech, silk-finish brass (4 grams)

5mm x 10mm rondelles, turquoise (2)

8mm x 12mm freshwater pearls, drilled lengthwise, buff (2)

10mm gold bead caps (2)
Clear glue
Gold topstitching thread
Memory wire (1½ coils)

#12 steel crochet hook
Masking tape
Wire cutters, heavy-duty

Bracelet Instructions

1. Refer to Counting from Patterns on page 17. Following Snake Bracelet Pattern Detail, thread on 30 repeats.

2. Crochet in a 10-around tube until you run out of beads. Bind off; bury the tails of both ends in the fibers of the tube.

3. Carefully slip memory wire through the tube, inching it forward through the center. It may be necessary to pull back a bit if the memory wire gets stuck in the threads inside the tube. When the wire emerges from the end of the tube, place a piece of masking tape on the end so it will not slip out again.

Snake Bracelet Pattern Overview

Snake Bracelet Pattern Detail

4. Slip one bead cap and one turquoise bead onto the wire at

End Bead Diagram

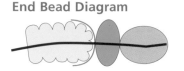

the other end. Check the fit of the pearls before proceeding. They should require a small amount of force to slide them on the end of the wire. Following End Bead Diagram, make a subtle bend approximately ¼" from the end of the wire, then dip the end of the wire into glue. Slide the pearl in place, forcing it if necessary. Allow glue to dry thoroughly according to manufacturer's instructions before proceeding with the other side. Check the glued pearl; it should be firmly in place and unmovable.

5. At the remaining end of the tube, compress the crocheted tube by pushing it back on the wire. Add the bead cap and the turquoise bead. Make a subtle bend in the memory wire approximately ¼" beyond the turquoise bead and coat the wire at that point with glue. Slide the pearl over the wire until it is in position at the end of the assembled bracelet. Place tape on the wire to keep the pearl in place while the glue dries. When the glue is dry, use heavy-duty wire cutters to trim off the wire just at the end of the pearl.

Earring Materials

☐ 15o seed beads, Toho # 557F, matte galvanized gold (600)

☐ 15o seed beads, Miyuki #412, opaque turquoise (360)

☐ 15o seed beads, Toho #86, Miyuki #454, purple iris (120)

○ 2.5mm round beads, gold (2)

⬭ 3mm x 6mm turquoise rondelles (4)

6mm–7mm gold bead caps (4)
22-gauge gold beading wire, 5" (2)
Gold earring findings (2)
1¼" gold head pins (2)
Light gold topstitching thread

#13 steel crochet hook
Round-nosed pliers
Stick pen, narrow
Wire cutters

Earring Instructions

1. Refer to Counting from Patterns on page 17. Following Snake Earring Pattern Detail, thread on 30 repeats.

2. Crochet in six-around tube until all beads are used.

3. Bind off and bury both tails within the fibers of the tube.

4. Carefully thread one wire through tube. Add the bead caps at both ends of the tube.

5. Using wire cutters, cut wire to ⅜" on each end of tube.

6. Using round-nosed pliers, turn the ends of the wire into loops.

7. Place one round bead and two rondelles on head pin; cut excess wire to ⅜" and turn the excess into a loop.

8. Following Assembly Diagram, assemble the earring.

9. Wrap wired tube around a stick pen. (Fig. 1)

10. Repeat Steps 1–9 for second earring, wrapping the second wired tube around the stick pen in the opposite direction so the earrings will be symmetrical.

Snake Earring Pattern Detail

Snake Earring Pattern Overview

Assembly Diagram

Fig. 1

Necklace Rope Materials

■ 11o seed beads, Czech #59155, green iris (1 gram)

■ 8o seed beads, Toho #22, metallic bronze (4 grams)

■ 8o seed beads, Czech, matte metallic light bronze (25 grams)

■ 8o seed beads, Czech #63130, opaque green turquoise (10 grams)

◗ 10mm gold bead caps (2)

╱ 20mm stick pearl, coordinating color

#10 bronze perle cotton

#10 steel crochet hook

Necklace Rope Instructions

1. Refer to Counting from Patterns on page 17. Following Snake Necklace Rope Pattern Detail, thread on approximately 100" of beads.

2. Crochet in six-around tube until the rope is approximately 16".

3. Following the Loop Diagram, add beads to one end. Following Toggle Diagram, add beads to the remaining end.

4. Bury the excess thread within the fibers of the tube and trim the excess thread.

Snake Necklace Rope Pattern Detail

Snake Necklace Rope Pattern Overview

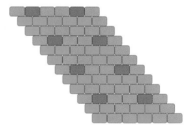

Toggle Diagram   **Loop Diagram**

Necklace Bail Materials

- 11o seed beads, Czech #59155, green iris (1 gram)
- 11o seed beads, Czech, light matte metallic bronze (2 grams)
- 11o seed beads, Czech #63130, opaque green turquoise (1 gram)
- 11o seed beads, Czech #25840, pale green silk (2 grams)
- 8o seed beads, Czech, light matte metallic bronze (3)
- 6mm turquoise rondelles
- 12mm turquoise disk with center-drilled hole
- 12mm oval pearl, beige

Necklace Bail Instructions

1. Refer to Brick Stitch on pages 27–28. Following Bail Pattern, work in brick stitch.

2. When the pattern is complete, fold the piece in half and secure the lower diagonal edges together with invisible stitches.

3. Following Bail Assembly Diagram, use an 8o seed bead to anchor the 12mm turquoise disk on the center front of the folded piece. Bring the thread out at the base point and add the pearl and turquoise drop.

4. Slip the bail onto the finished rope.

Bail Assembly Diagram

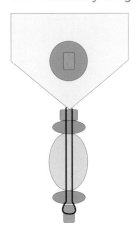

Bail Pattern

rainbow bangle

Materials

- 8o seed beads, Czech #63030, opaque aqua (13 per repeat)
- 8o seed beads, Czech #93110, opaque light orange (13 per repeat)
- 8o seed beads, Czech #53410, opaque lime (13 per repeat)
- 8o seed beads, Czech #33210, opaque medium blue (13 per repeat)
- 8o seed beads, Czech #53250, opaque medium green (13 per repeat)
- 8o seed beads, Czech #83130, opaque yellow (13 per repeat)

#10 ivory perle cotton

#10 steel crochet hook

Instructions

Note: This bangle has a complex repeat, consisting of 13 rounds.

1. Refer to Counting from Patterns on page 17. Following Rainbow Pattern Detail, thread on enough full repeats to create a length of approximately 45".

2. Crochet in six-around tube until all the beads are used.

3. Refer to Making an Invisible Join on pages 20–21. Join the two ends invisibly.

Rainbow Pattern Overview

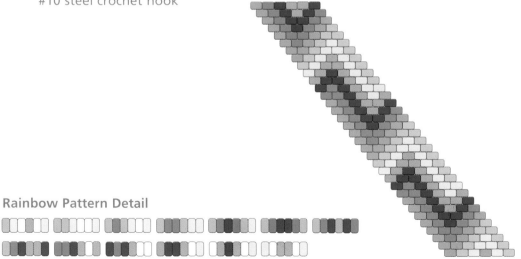

Rainbow Pattern Detail

leopard spots bracelet

Materials

- 11o seed beads, Toho #610F or Miyuki #401F, matte black (2 grams)
- 11o seed beads, Toho #557F, matte galvanized gold (3 grams)
- 11o seed beads, Czech #13600M, matte opaque chestnut (2 grams)
- 11o seed beads, Czech opaque bone (3 grams)
- 11o seed beads, Czech silk-finish light copper (2 grams)
- 10mm x 15mm faceted focal stone, mookite or crazy-lace agate

7mm copper bead caps (2)

Ochre topstitching thread

#11 steel crochet hook

Instructions

1. Refer to Counting from Patterns on page 17. Following Leopard Spots Pattern Detail, thread on 11 repeats to create a 6½" tube.

2. Crochet in an eight-around tube until you have achieved the desired length; bind off, leaving an 8" tail. Bury the tail at the starting end in the fibers of the tube.

3. Refer to Finishing with a Focal Bead on pages 21–22. Finish with the bead caps and faceted focal stone.

Leopard Spots Pattern Overview

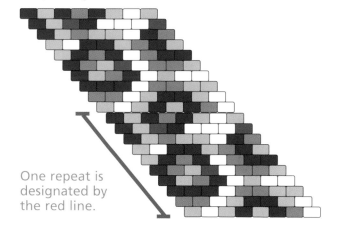

One repeat is designated by the red line.

Leopard Spots Pattern Detail

diamonds bangle

designed by Edith Allison

Materials

- 11o seed beads, Toho #45AF, matte opaque dark red (8 per repeat)

- 11o seed beads, Toho #2032, matte opaque olive (14 per repeat)

- 11o seed beads, Miyuki #149F, matte transparent capri blue (26 per repeat)

- 11o seed beads, Toho #413, opaque lustered AB turquoise (51 per repeat)

Ivory topstitching thread

#11 steel crochet hook

Instructions

1. Refer to Counting from Patterns on page 17. Following Diamonds Pattern Detail, thread on number of repeats for desired measurement.

Note: Eight repeats of the pattern will make a roll-on bangle that will fit a 6½" wrist.

2. Crochet in seven-around tube until all the beads are used.

3. Refer to Making an Invisible Join on pages 20–21. Join the two ends invisibly.

Diamonds Pattern Detail

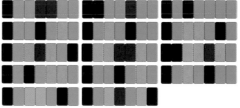

Diamonds Pattern Overview

sugar & spice bangle

designed by Edith Allison

Materials

- 11o seed beads, Miyuki #19F, matte transparent purple (6 per repeat)
- 11o seed beads, Miyuki #141F, matte transparent ruby (54 per repeat)
- 11o seed beads, Miyuki #1981, steel plated (24 per repeat)

Gray topstitching thread

#11 steel crochet hook

Instructions

1. Refer to Counting from Patterns on page 17. Following Sugar & Spice Pattern Detail, thread on number of repeats for desired measurement.

Note: Seven repeats of the pattern will make a roll-on bangle that will fit a 6½" wrist.

2. Crochet in six-around tube until all the beads are used.

3. Refer to Making an Invisible Join on pages 20–21. Join the two ends invisibly.

Sugar & Spice Pattern Detail

Sugar & Spice Pattern Overview

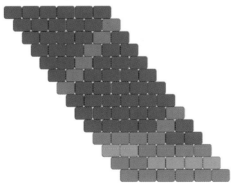

sweet dreams bangle

designed by Pat McMullan

Materials

- 11o seed beads, Miyuki #401F, matte opaque black (26 per repeat)
- 11o seed beads, Miyuki #149F, matte transparent capri blue (26 per repeat)
- 11o seed beads, Miyuki #338, silver-lined dark capri blue (26 per repeat)

Blue topstitching thread

#11 steel crochet hook

Instructions

1. Refer to Counting from Patterns on page 17. Following Sweet Dreams Pattern Detail, thread enough repeats to create desired length.

Note: Eleven repeats of the pattern will make a roll-on bangle that will fit a 6½" wrist.

2. Crochet in six-around tube until all the beads are used.

3. Refer to Making an Invisible Join on pages 20–21. Join the two ends invisibly.

Sweet Dreams Pattern Detail

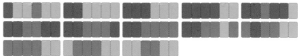

Sweet Dreams Pattern Overview

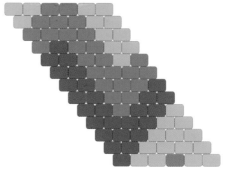

triangle treat bangle

designed by Pat McMullan

Materials

- 11o seed beads, Miyuki #401F, matte opaque black (5 per repeat)
- 11o seed beads, Toho #2078, matte opaque light blue (8 per repeat)
- 11o seed beads, Toho #401F, matte opaque white (12 per repeat)
- 11o seed beads, Miyuki #149F, matte transparent capri blue (8 per repeat)

Blue topstitching thread

#11 steel crochet hook

Instructions

1. Refer to Counting from Patterns on page 17. Following Triangle Treat Pattern Detail, thread enough repeats to create desired length.

Note: Nine repeats of the pattern will make a roll-on bangle that will fit a 6½" wrist.

2. Crochet in seven-around tube until all the beads are used.

3. Refer to Making an Invisible Join on pages 20–21. Join the two ends invisibly.

Triangle Treat Pattern Detail

Triangle Treat Pattern Overview

flower girl bracelet

Materials

- 11o seed beads, Miyuki #520 or Toho #144, Ceylon light green (8 per repeat)
- 11o seed beads, Toho #145, Ceylon pink (16 per repeat)
- 11o seed beads, Czech #53250, opaque dark green (14 per repeat)
- 11o seed beads, Miyuki #408A or Czech #93210, opaque dark red (2 per repeat)
- 11o seed beads, Miyuki #420 or Toho #121 or Czech #46102, opaque luster white (34 per repeat)
- 11o seed beads, Miyuki #411 or Czech #53200, opaque medium green (4 per repeat)
- 11o seed beads, Toho #125 or Czech #93190, opaque medium red (8 per repeat)

#10 white perle cotton

#10 steel crochet hook

Instructions

1. Refer to Counting from Patterns on page 17. Following Flower Girl Detail, thread on enough repeats to create a 48" length. This will create a bracelet of about 6½".

> *Note: To lengthen or shorten, add or subtract full repeats only.*

2. Crochet in six-around tube until all beads are used.

3. Bind off, leaving a 10" tail.

4. Bury the starting tail within the fibers of the tube. Refer to Making an Invisible Join on pages 20–21. Use the ending tail to join two ends invisibly.

5. Bury the excess ending tail within the fibers of the tube and clip closely.

Flower Girl Pattern Overview

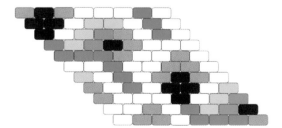

Flower Girl Pattern Detail

crystal secrets bangle

Materials

- 11o seed beads, Czech #68150, copper-lined crystal (4 per repeat)
- 11o seed beads, Czech #01750 or Toho #514F, matte dark copper (3 per repeat)
- 11o seed beads, Toho #21 or Miyuki #1 or Czech #78102, silver-lined crystal (4 per repeat)
- 3mm fire-polish beads, vitrail-finish (1 per repeat)

8mm x 12mm focal bead, silver

7mm–8mm silver bead caps (2)

Light gray topstitching thread

#10 steel crochet hook

Instructions

1. Refer to Counting from Patterns on page 17. Following Crystal Secrets Pattern Detail, thread on enough repeats to equal the measurement of the wrist size minus ½".

2. Crochet in a six-around tube until all beads are used; bind off, leaving an 8" tail. Bury the tail at the starting end in the fibers of the tube.

3. Refer to Finishing with a Focal Bead on pages 21–22. Finish with the bead caps and silver focal bead.

Crystal Secrets Pattern Detail

Crystal Secrets Pattern Overview

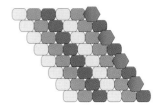

remember when

joined tubes & cabochons

argyle earrings

Materials

- 15o seed beads, Miyuki #2003, matte light olive (1 gram)
- 15o seed beads, Miyuki #2075, matte metallic cobalt (1 gram)
- 15o seed beads, Toho #557 or Miyuki #277, metallic gold (2 grams)
- 15o seed beads, Miyuki #2076, matte metallic red (1 gram)
- 15o seed beads, Miyuki #410B, opaque dark amethyst (1 gram)
- 8mm x 5mm fire-polish faceted rondelle, matte olive (2)

- 5mm gold bead caps, conical shape (4)
- Gold ear wires, open-ended (2)
- 1¼" gold head pins (2)
- Ochre topstitching thread

- #13 steel crochet hook
- Round-nosed pliers
- Wire cutters

Instructions

1. Refer to Counting from Patterns on page 17. Following Argyle Pattern Detail, thread on 14 repeats.

Argyle Pattern Detail

Argyle Pattern Overview

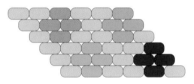

2. Crochet tube; bind off and bury both tails within the fibers of the tube.

3. Slide 48 metallic gold 15o seed beads onto a new thread. Refer to Joining Two Tube Ends to Reduce to One on page 22. Pull up a new loop on the taped-together tube tops. Crochet two rounds of 10 beads each.

4. Reduce two beads in the third round by making a slip stitch without a bead; the third round will have eight beads.

5. Work another round of eight beads, then reduce by two more beads; this round will have six beads.

6. Work one more round of six beads.

7. Slip-stitch without beads all around the top edge to force the beads of the last round into a horizontal position.

8. Bind off; bury the tail within the fibers of the reduction area.

9. Following Assembly Diagram, assemble the earring. Force the head pin up into the joined tube until it is securely caught within the fibers of the reduction area, but does not pull through. Add the bead cap. Make a wrapped loop with the head pin that forces the bead cap onto the top of the reduction area.

Assembly Diagram

10. Cut off excess wire and flatten the cut end.

11. Slip the rondelle and the bead cap onto the open end of the ear wire. Trim the excess end to ⅜" and make a loop at the base of the cap. Join the lower section to the loop before closing.

12. Repeat Steps 1–11 for second earring.

spumoni bracelet

Several links are worked continuously to create this bracelet. One long thread is used to hold the central beads within the center of each link.

Materials

- 11o seed beads, Czech #68506, copper-lined crystal (10 grams)
- 11o seed beads, Toho #560F, matte galvanized light green (20 grams)
- 11o seed beads, Czech #78030, opaque lustered pink (20 grams)
- 8o seed beads, Miyuki #2035, matte metallic light olive AB (5 grams)
- 12mm x 20mm focal beads (4–5 depending on bracelet length)
- 8mm copper bead caps (2)
- Copper clasp and ring
- Pink topstitching thread (3 spools)
- #11 steel crochet hook

Instructions

Note: You will make several different threadings to create this bracelet.

1. Thread on beads. For the first threading, thread on 54 pink 11o beads, six copper-lined 11o beads, 54 light green 11o beads, ten 8o beads, and 48 copper-lined 11o beads. (Fig. 1)

2. For the second threading, thread on 54 pink 11o beads, six copper-lined 11o beads, 54 light green 11o beads, ten 8o beads, 40 copper-lined 11o beads, ten 8o beads, 54 pink 11o beads, six copper-lined 11o beads, and 54 light green 11o beads.

3. Repeat Step 2 for third and fourth threadings.

4. For the final threading, thread on 48 copper-lined 11o beads, 54 pink 11o beads, six copper-lined 11o beads, and 54 green 11o beads.

Fig. 1

5. Using the first threading, crochet two rounds in six-around tube. Following Increase to Eight Diagram, increase by two beads in the next round by making a chain stitch with one bead.

Increase to Eight Diagram

 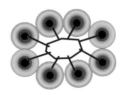

Making a chain stitch with one bead

Increased beads fit into the round

6. Work another round of eight until there are four complete rounds, and the top round has eight beads.

7. Following Increase to Ten Diagram, increase by two beads in the next round in the same manner.

Increase to Ten Diagram

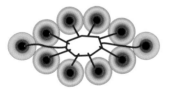 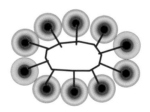

Making a chain stitch with one bead

Increased beads fit into the round

8. Add one more round so you have a total of six rounds, and the top round has ten beads. At this point you should have used all the copper-lined 11o beads.

9. Crochet one round of 8o beads.

10. Following New Tube Diagram, chain one with a green bead. Continue in counter-clockwise direction, adding five more green beads until you have a total of six green beads. You will have created a separate green tube of six around.

New Tube Diagram

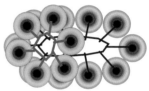

11. Continue crocheting in six-around tube until you have used all the beads.

12. Return to the point where the first separate green tube was created, and create a second green tube. Pull in a loop using the second thread. Chain one with a green bead, then continue around as previously described until the pink beads are used, and you have a second separate tube the same length as the first.

13. Refer to Joining Two Tube Ends to Reduce to One on page 22. Tape the ends of the two tubes together. Add one round of ten 8o beads.

14. Add four rounds of ten copper-lined 11o beads and one more round of 8o beads.

15. Split off a separate tube of six around as you did previously. Crochet in six around until you have used all the beads of the second threading. Continue as previously, until the bracelet just fits around the wrist.

16. Bring in the final threading as the other side of the last separate tube. Tape the ends together as you did previously; crochet three rounds of ten.

17. Decrease two beads in the next round, then crochet another round of eight. Decrease two beads in the next round, then crochet another round of six.

18. Bind off, leaving a 15" tail for finishing.

19. Bury the starting thread, and any other tail threads from joinings.

20. Bring the ending thread out from the center of the bound off tube. Add one bead cap. Add four copper-lined 11o beads, then run the beaded thread through one end of the clasp or ring. Run the thread back through the cap and into the tube, then out at the point where the pink tubes separate.

21. Add one 8o bead, one focal bead, and one more 8o bead. Run the thread through the joint made of 8o beads and copper-lined 11o beads, then bring it out at the point where the next two pink tubes separate. Continue until the thread emerges from the starting end.

22. Add the bead cap. **Fig. 2** Add four copper-lined 11o beads, then join the other end of the clasp or ring. (Fig. 2)

23. Reinforce the entire bracelet with a second run of thread, including the beaded loops that attach the ring and clasp. Secure the thread within the fibers of the tube and bury the thread end in the tube.

lemon blossom necklace

Materials

- 15o seed beads, Toho #221, metallic bronze (2 grams)
- Delica beads, Miyuki #21 or Toho #221, metallic bronze (2 grams)
- 11o seed beads, Toho #560F, matte galvanized light green (10 grams)
- 11o seed beads, Toho #221, metallic bronze (30 grams)
- 11o seed beads, Czech #03152, pale green opaque (20 grams)
- 6mm pearls, bronze (2)
- 6mm x 8mm fire-polish faceted rondelles, green/bronze (7)
- 8mm fire-polish faceted round, bronze

30mm x 40mm lemon chrysophase cabochon, irregular oval-shaped

Gold bead caps (2)

Gold chain medium-weight (6")

Gold lobster claw clasp

Medium brown topstitching thread

#11 steel crochet hook

Instructions

1. Refer to Counting from Patterns on page 17. Following Surround Pattern Detail, thread on enough repeats to create a 40" length.

2. Crochet in six-around tube until there is an even number of rounds that fit closely around the cabochon.

3. Refer to Surrounding a Cabochon on pages 24–26. Add one ridge row of bronze 11o seed beads.

4. Refer to Making an Invisible Join on pages 20–21. Align the ends and join the tube invisibly.

5. Add a second ridge row of bronze 11o seed beads. Add delicas and 15o seed beads to enclose the cabochon.

Surround Pattern Detail

Surround Pattern Overview

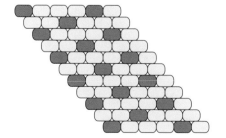

6. Following Neckband Pattern Detail, thread on enough repeats to create a 60" length for the neckband.

7. Crochet in six-around tube until the tube is approximately 12" long.

8. Bind off and bury the starting and ending tails within the fibers of the tube.

9. Make a small hook out of the wire and insert the hooked end into the end of the tube. Pull back until the hook catches in the fibers of the tube. Following the Necklace End Diagram, slip the caps in place and attach the chain to both ends in 3" section. Add the lobster claw clasp to one end and the additional rondelle to the other.

10. Determine the location for the hanging bail. Create a limited ridge for the bail, nine beads in width, in the same manner as for the full sur-round bail. Refer to Peyote Stitch on pages 26–27. Add in four beads, then work in peyote stitch until the bail is long enough.

11. Add one row of beads along the edge to cre-ate the necessary width. Attach the bail to the back of the surround with invisible stitches. (Fig. 1) Bury the excess thread within the weave and clip close.

12. Add the pearls and 8mm fire-polish beads as decorations at the bail attachment point. (Fig. 2)

Neckband Pattern Detail

Neckband Pattern Overview

Necklace End Diagram

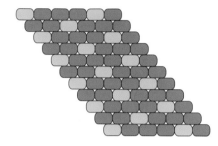

Fig. 1

Fig. 2

tea party necklace

tea party necklace

This necklace is another good example of the harmonious interaction between beads and fibers. The variegated metallic fiber used to create the tube is both softened and enhanced by the transparent 8o seed beads.

Materials

11o seed bead, gold

8o seed beads, transparent crystal AB (50 grams)

4mm faceted round crystals or fire-polish beads (8)

6mm gold spacer

8mm faceted round crystal or fire-polish bead

8mm gold beads (2)

10mm faceted round crystal or fire-polish bead

12mm faceted rondelle

18mm x 25mm faceted amethyst drop bead

20mm flat square turquoise bead

Variegated metallic braid, light-weight

#10 steel crochet hook

Instructions

Note: This necklace can be made in any length without concern for pattern.

1. Thread on enough beads to achieve the desired length. You will use 60 per inch of rope.

2. Crochet in six-around tube.

Note: The necklace should slip over your head without findings, so check the fit before finishing. If necessary, add more thread and beads until you have the correct length.

3. Refer to Joining Two Tube Ends to Reduce to One on page 22. Join the two ends together into one. Slip stitch without a bead in the last round.

4. Bring a new thread out from the center of the joined end of the rope.

5. Set aside the 4mm faceted crystals or fire-polish beads.

6. Following Drop Assembly Diagram, add the larger beads in the order shown. Skip the 11o at the end and run the thread back through all the beads; reinforce with a second pass of thread.

7. When the pendant is secure, surround the point where the rope ends and the drop begins with a ring of 4mm faceted crystals or fire-polish beads.

Drop Assembly Diagram

Ring of 4mm faceted crystals

12mm faceted rondelle

18mm x 25mm faceted amethyst drop bead

8mm gold bead

10mm faceted round crystal

8mm gold bead

20mm flat square bead

6mm gold spacer

8mm faceted round crystal

11o gold seed bead

What it's like when you're big...

looking glass necklace

Materials

- 15o seed beads, Toho # 557, galvanized metallic gold (2 grams)
- 12o three-cut beads, Czech #18389, galvanized metallic gold (8 grams)
- Delica beads, #61, lustered transparent raspberry (3 grams)
- 4mm bicones, opal glass (16)
- 6mm bicones, medium amethyst (10)
- 8mm x 10mm fire opal
- 8mm x 10mm freshwater pearls, dusty raspberry (5)
- 30 mm x 40 mm opalescent glass cabochon
- Gold beading wire, nylon-coated, lightweight (18")
- Gold clasp and ring
- Gold crimps
- Gold topstitching thread
- #13 steel crochet hook

Instructions

1. Refer to Surrounding a Cabochon on pages 24–26. Create the pattern for the surrounding tube by alternating 12o three-cuts and delica beads: raspberry, gold, raspberry, gold, to create a tight spiral pattern. Thread on 240 repeats of raspberry and gold.

Note: This will be enough beads for 80 rounds of six.

2. Crochet in six-around tube. When you near the end of the beads, check the fit of the tube around the cabochon. When you have enough rounds in an even number to fit neatly around the cabochon, stop crocheting and bind off.

Note: If you began the tube with a raspberry bead, you should end with a gold bead.

3. Bury the starting tail.

4. Bring up a "peyote" ridge row using gold 12o three-cuts.

5. Refer to Making an Invisible Join on pages 20–21. Align the ends and join the tube invisibly.

6. Finish the ridges in gold 12o seed beads and 15o seed beads, reducing as needed to enclose the cabochon.

7. Following Bail #1–Bail #4 diagrams, pick up a ridge of three beads in a similar manner as used to create the peyote ridge for the cabochon surround to create the bail. The first three diagrams show the bail as six beads wide. The final bail should be seven beads wide. Refer to Peyote Stitch on pages 26–27. Complete the required length in peyote stitch, then add one row along the side of the bail to make it symmetrical.

Bail #1 Diagram

Bail #3 Diagram

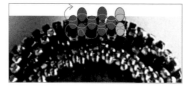

Bail #2 Diagram

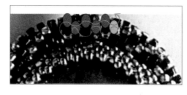

Bail #4 Diagram

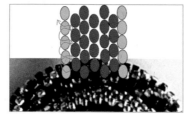

8. Sew the central embellishment bead over the bail attachment point.

9. Thread the wire through the bail. Add enough 12o seed beads to cover the wire that runs through the bail.

10. Following Strand Assembly Diagram, thread on the beads of the strand, starting at the bottom with one dusty raspberry pearl.

11. Attach the clasp and ring.

Strand Assembly Diagram

Clasp/ring

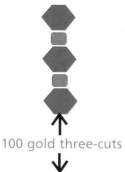

100 gold three-cuts

seaside necklace

In this design, three separate six-around tubes are joined together to form one necklace. The pattern is different for each tube, but all three are coordinated in design theme and in color.

Materials

80 seed beads, Toho #180F, frosted transparent green iris (30 grams)

80 seed beads, Toho #558F, matte light gold (10 grams)

80 seed beads, Czech, matte metallic bronze (40 grams)

6mm round beads, tigereye (2)

30mm round donut, center-drilled hole, aventurine

#8 or #10 medium tan perle cotton (25 grams)

Tan nylon beading thread, lightweight

18-gauge gold beading wire (4")

#10 steel crochet hook

Round-nosed pliers

Instructions

1. Refer to Counting from Patterns on page 17. Following Three-tube Short Pattern Detail, thread on 31 repeats to equal a length of 15".

2. Following Three-tube Medium Pattern Detail on page 112, thread on 198 repeats to equal a length of 17½".

3. Following Three-tube Long Pattern Detail on page 112, thread on 105 repeats to equal a length of 20".

Three-tube Short Pattern Overview

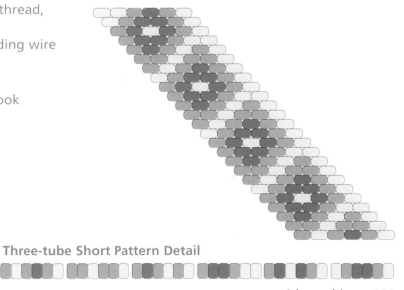

Three-tube Short Pattern Detail

4. Crochet each of the three tubes until they are the desired lengths.

5. Refer to Joining Three Tube Ends to Reduce to One on pages 23–24. Join the three tubes together and reduce to six beads per round. Crochet one round of slip stitch without beads to properly position the end beads to horizontal orientation, the same as the beads of the tubes and the reduction area.

6. Bind off and bury the tails of both ends within the fibers of the reduced ends.

7. To create the wire clasp, bend the wire in half at the center. Following Bending Diagram and using round-nosed pliers, make a hook near the bend point. Make a gentle curve along the center of the length of the wire, but curve it sharply at the open end.

Note: The hook you create at the open end will hold the clasp in place.

8. Following Clasp Diagram, insert the open end of the clasp in one end and push it into the tube until the full length except the top curve is inside the tube. Pull up so the hook at the open end catches in the fibers of the reduction.

9. Thread a needle with a doubled strand of the lightweight beading nylon and bring a thread out in the center of the last round of the reduction at the other end. Following Toggle Diagram, sew the donut and 6mm beads in place. Make a second pass of thread to reinforce the assembly. Bury the excess thread in the fiber of the tube.

Three-tube Medium Pattern Overview

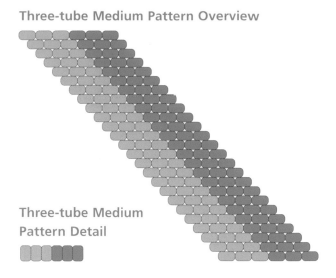

Three-tube Medium Pattern Detail

Three-tube Long Pattern Overview

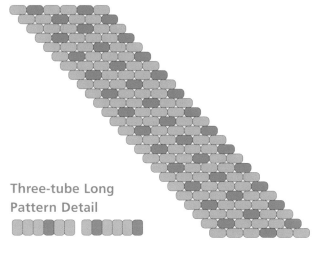

Three-tube Long Pattern Detail

Bending Diagram   **Clasp Diagram**   **Toggle Diagram**

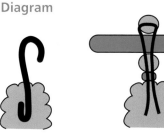

putting on the ritz

chain stitch patterns

pearly girl necklace

This pattern arose from a happy accident—I wanted to crochet a smooth chain with the gold flexible wire, thinking it would create the illusion of actual metal chain. To my delighted surprise, it began to coil after just a few stitches; the result was pleasing chaos! Don't be tempted to try to straighten out the wire—just let it do its thing. You'll be pleasantly surprised. No two of these necklaces will be exactly alike.

Materials
6mm–10mm cupped pearls, center-drilled (38)

8mm–10mm beads, large-holed, gold (2)

Large central pearl, top-drilled

Gold beading wire, lightweight flexible (6 yards)

Gold crimps (4)

Gold toggle set

#10 steel crochet hook
Round-nosed pliers

Instructions
1. Cleanly trim the end of the wire, then slip 19 cupped pearls on the wire, followed by the large central pearl. Add the remaining 19 cupped pearls.

2. Leave a starting tail of approximately 2". Take up the slack in each stitch as you progress; you will not be able to do so after the next stitch. Crochet as follows:
Ch 60, ch 1 with pearl, ch 15, ch 1 with pearl, ch 15, ch 1 with pearl, ch 114, ch 1 with pearl, ch 13, ch 1 with pearl. Continue in this pattern, decreasing the number of chs between each ch 1 with pearl by one each time. When you get to the point where you are chaining only 1 between pearls, continue in this manner until you have chained with all the cupped pearls before the central pearl. Ch 2, ch 1 with central pearl, leaving enough slack in the ch so

the pearl hangs freely. Ch 2, ch 1 with pearl, then repeat the pattern in reverse on the previous side. End with ch 60. Bind off by pulling the wire all the way through the last loop.

3. Following Toggle Diagram, assemble each end. Slide one crimp on the wire, followed by the large gold bead. Add the second crimp and half of the toggle. Run the wire back through the second crimp, the gold bead, and the first crimp. Using crimping pliers, flatten the crimps to hold the wire. Run the excess wire through the first several chains, then trim, taking care not to cut the wire of the necklace.

Toggle Diagram

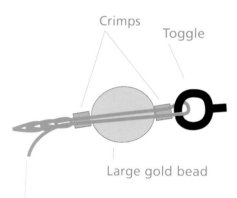

Crimps

Toggle

Large gold bead

Bury this extra wire in the first several chains of the necklace, then trim, taking care not to cut the wire of the necklace.

Some days you just feel like a princess.

fairy-tale necklace

fairy-tale necklace

Materials

12o three-cut beads, Toho #539
(6 grams)

8o seed beads, Czech #59135 purple
iris (7 grams)

6mm round fire-polish faceted
beads, light amethyst AB (7 grams)

6mm round glass beads, medium
purple (18)

7mm x 12mm leaf beads top-drilled,
Czech, vitrail-finish olive (6)

8mm round fire-polish faceted
beads, Czech, peridot (3)

8mm silver split rings (2)

Silver S-hook clasp

28-gauge olive beading wire (20
yards)

16-gauge silver beading wire (18")

#10 steel crochet hook

Round-nosed pliers

Wire cutters

Instructions

1. Thread beads onto the olive wire in this order: *Seventy-nine 12o three-cut beads, nine 8o seed beads, one 6mm round faceted fire-polish bead, nine 8o seed beads*, repeat between *s five more times, seventy-nine 12o three-cut beads, **one Czech leaf bead, three 6mm round glass beads, one 8mm round faceted fire-polish bead, three 6mm round glass beads**, one Czech leaf bead, five 8o seed beads, repeat between **s once more, one Czech leaf bead, three 6mm round glass beads, one 8mm round faceted fire-polish bead, three 6mm round glass beads, one Czech leaf bead, *seventy-nine 12o three-cut beads, nine 8o seed beads, one 6mm round faceted fire-polish bead, nine 8o seed beads*, repeat between *s five more times, seventy-nine 12o three-cut beads.

2. Stitch as follows: Leaving a 3" tail, ch 12 without beads to a length of approximately 1¼". [Slip 12o three-cut beads in the next 15 ch as follows: 2 in first chain, 3 in next, 4 in next, then 5, 6, 7, 8, 9, 8, 7, 6, 5, 4, 3, 2 in subsequent chains. ***Slip five 8o seed beads in next ch, slip four 8o seed beads in next ch***.

Ch 1 with 6mm round faceted fire-polish bead, three times. Repeat between ***s. Make a slip stitch to join the last cluster of 8o seed beads with the first cluster of 8o seed beads.] Repeat between [ ]s five more times. Slip 12o three-cut beads in the next 15 ch as follows: 2 in first chain, 3 in next, 4 in next, then 5, 6, 7, 8, 9, 8, 7, 6, 5, 4, 3, 2 in subsequent chains.

#Ch 1 with Czech leaf beads, ch 1 with three 6mm round glass beads, ch 1 with 8mm round faceted fire-polish bead, ch 1 with three 6mm round glass beads, ch 1 with Czech leaf bead, ch 1 with 8o seed bead, five times#. Repeat between #s. Ch 1 with Czech leaf bead, ch 1 with three 6mm round glass beads, ch 1 with 8mm round faceted fire-polish bead, ch 1 with three 6mm round glass beads, ch 1 with Czech leaf beads. [Slip 12o three-cut beads in the next 15 ch as follows: 2 in first chain, 3 in next, 4 in next, then 5, 6, 7, 8, 9, 8, 7, 6, 5, 4, 3, 2 in subsequent chains. ***Slip five 8o seed beads in next ch, sl four 8o seed beads in next ch***. Ch 1 with 6mm round faceted fire-polish bead, three times. Repeat between ***s. Make a slip stitch to join the last cluster of 8o seed beads with the first cluster of 8o seed beads.] Repeat between [ ]s five more times. Slip 12o three-cut beads in the next 15 ch as follows: 2 in first chain, 3 in next, 4 in next, then 5, 6, 7, 8, 9, 8,

7, 6, 5, 4, 3, 2 in subsequent chains. End with 12 ch without beads. Bind off the end wire, leaving a 3" tail.

3. Using round-nosed pliers, make a curve at each end of the silver wire. Use approximately 1" of the wire at both ends of the 16-gauge wire so the resulting necklace is approximately 16".

4. Wrap one end of the beaded olive wire around the interior and exterior curves of the loop until it is secure. Bury the tail within the first 12 ch and trim the tail.

5. Using a smooth motion, wrap the entire beaded chain around the silver wire so the three groups with 8mm center beads land in the middle. Arrange the beads so the effect is frilly and close. Some of the silver wire will show through the beaded chain. Continue wrapping until reaching the remaining loop end of silver wire.

6. Secure the remaining end of the olive wire around the loop in the same manner as for the first loop. Secure the tail within the chains and trim. Shift the wrapped beaded chain as necessary to arrive at a pleasing appearance.

7. Attach the split rings and S-hook onto the loops to finish the necklace.

sparkly bracelet

Materials

4mm fire-polish crystals, silver-finish (240)

12mm–15mm beads, large-holed, silver (2)

Silver metallic braid, medium-weight, (20 yards)

20-gauge silver beading wire (12")

#9 steel crochet hook

Clear glue

Round-nosed pliers

Wire cutters

Instructions

1. Thread approximately half of 4mm fire-polish beads onto one spool of braid. When this spool is depleted, thread remaining beads onto the second spool. Leave a beginning and ending tail of 4" on each strand to be used later in tying the strands together.

2. Crochet eight strands, each as follows: Ch5, then *ch1 with bead, ch5*, repeat between *s until the crocheted part measures 2½" larger than the wrist. Bind off, leaving a 4" thread tail for finishing.

3. Lay all strands out on a flat surface and arrange them so the start and end of the chain crochet lines up evenly. (Fig. 1)

Fig. 1

4. Using your crochet hook (non-hook end), tie the strands together with the thread tails at both ends to position the knot as

Fig. 2

close to the end of the chain crochet as possible. (Fig. 2 on page 122)

5. Saturate the knot with glue, tighten the knot, and allow to dry. Trim tails to ¼" on both ends. (Fig. 3)

Fig. 3

6. Measure the wrist. Leave 2" at one end of the wire, then wrap the wire twice around the knot at one end of the tied bunch of strands. (Fig. 4)

Fig. 4

7. Compress the wrap and knot with pliers. Wrap the whole bunch of strands continuously around the wire until the spiraled section, from knot to knot, is the same length as the wrist measurement. Wrap the wire around the knot at that point; compress the wrap and knot with pliers.

8. Slide the large-holed beads over the wrapped knots and trim the excess wire to 1½".

9. Following Spiral Diagram and using pliers, form a spiral in the end of the wire.

Spiral Diagram

10. Gently bend the entire assembly into the shape of the wrist.

confetti necklace

Materials

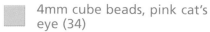 3mm round silver-plated metal beads (44)

 4mm cube beads, pink cat's eye (34)

6mm heart beads, light green cat's eye (22)

6mm star beads, light blue cat's eye (52)

18mm silver end cones (2)

1½" 24-gauge silver beading wire (2)

Silver S-hook clasp

Variegated pastel metallic braid, very fine

#10 steel crochet hook

Clear glue

Round-nosed pliers

Wire cutters

Assembly Diagram

Instructions

1. Leaving a 4" tail at the beginning and end of each strand, work all strands according to the patterns given below; bind off at the end of each strand. Each finished strand should measure approximately 19".

Strand 1 (make two)
Thread on seventeen 4mm cubes. Ch 15, *ch 1 with cube, chain 10*, repeat between *s until you reach the last cube, end with ch 15.

Strand 2 (make two)
Thread on twenty-six 6mm stars. *Ch 7, ch 1 with star*, repeat between *s until all the stars are crocheted, end with ch 7.

Strand 3 (make two)
Thread on twenty-two 3mm round beads. *Ch 8, ch 1 with bead*, repeat between *s until all the beads are crocheted, end with ch 8.

Strand 4 (make two)
Thread on eleven 6mm hearts. *Ch 16, ch 1 with heart*, repeat between *s until all the hearts are crocheted, end with ch 16.

2. Line up all the strands together in any order so the ends match up. Gather all the strands together and, using a needle to guide the knot into position, tie a knot at each end so the knot lands very close to the end of the chain. Dab a spot of glue on the knot before tightening. When the glue is dry on the tightened knot, trim the excess tail threads to no more than ⅜".

3. Following Assembly Diagram, add end cones and clasp.

about the author

photo courtesy of Bertelsman Publishing

Biography

Ann Benson has been beading for more than a quarter of a century and has written many previous books on beading, including *Beadweaving*, *Beadwork Basics*, *Two-Hour Beaded Projects*, *Beading for the First Time*, *Beadpoint*, and *The New Beadweaving*. She lives in Connecticut with her husband and is the mother of two grown daughters. She is also the author of several published novels, including *The Plague Tales*, *The Burning Road* and *Thief of Souls*.

Dedication

This book is dedicated to my husband Gary.

Acknowledgments

Thanks to the many stitchers who helped in the creation of the projects in this book: Tina Harley, Dana Monaco, and Elda Frisina. Pat McMullan and Edith Allison provided important design and technique advice as the projects unfolded, as well as designs for specific projects, for which I am grateful. Denise Doyon is responsible for my addiction to beaded crochet, for which I thank her. Renee Frost kept my bead life organized while a maelstrom of crochet chaos whirled around us; her contribution to the completion of this work is immeasurably appreciated.

PO Box 1315
Manchester CT 06066
www.beadseast.com
info@beadseast.com

acknowledgments

Photography for this book was done by Ryne Hazen for Hazen Photography.

metric chart

mm-millimeters   cm-centimeters
INCHES TO MILLIMETERS AND CENTIMETERS

inches	mm	cm	inches	cm	inches	cm
⅛	3	0.3	9	22.9	30	76.2
¼	6	0.6	10	25.4	31	78.7
½	13	1.3	12	30.5	33	83.8
⅝	16	1.6	13	33.0	34	86.4
¾	19	1.9	14	35.6	35	88.9
⅞	22	2.2	15	38.1	36	91.4
1	25	2.5	16	40.6	37	94.0
1¼	32	3.2	17	43.2	38	96.5
1½	38	3.8	18	45.7	39	99.1
1¾	44	4.4	19	48.3	40	101.6
2	51	5.1	20	50.8	41	104.1
2½	64	6.4	21	53.3	42	106.7
3	76	7.6	22	55.9	43	109.2
3½	89	8.9	23	58.4	44	111.8
4	102	10.2	24	61.0	45	114.3
4½	114	11.4	25	63.5	46	116.8
5	127	12.7	26	66.0	47	119.4
6	152	15.2	27	68.6	48	121.9
7	178	17.8	28	71.1	49	124.5
8	203	20.3	29	73.7	50	127.0

index